Claiming Victory: A Romantic Comedy

The Dartmouth Diaries Book One

Beverley Watts

BaR Publishing

Cover design by Berni Stevens at bernistevenscoverdesign.com

Contents

Chapter One

Retired Admiral, Charles Shackleford, entered the dimly lit interior of his favourite watering hole. Once inside, he waited a second for his eyes to adjust, and glanced around to check that his ageing Springer spaniel was already seated beside his stool at the bar. Pickles had disappeared into the undergrowth half a mile back, as they walked along the wooded trail high above the picturesque River Dart. The scent of some poor unfortunate rabbit had caught his still youthful nose. The Admiral was not unduly worried; this was a regular occurrence, and Pickles knew his way to the Ship Inn better than his master.

Satisfied that all was as it should be for a Friday lunchtime, Admiral Shackleford waved to the other regulars, and made his way to his customary seat at the bar where his long standing, and long suffering friend, Jimmy Noon, was already halfway down his first pint.

'You're a bit late today Sir,' observed Jimmy, after saluting his former commanding officer smartly.

Charles Shackleford grunted as he heaved his ample bottom onto the bar stool. 'Got bloody waylaid by that bossy daughter of mine.' He sighed dramatically before taking a long draft of his pint of real ale, which was ready and waiting for him. 'Damn bee in her bonnet since she found out about my relationship with Mabel Pomfrey. Of course, I told her to mind her own bloody business, but it has to be said that the cat's out of the bag, and no mistake.'

He stared gloomily down into his pint. 'She said it cast aspersions on her poor mother's memory. But what she doesn't understand Jimmy, is that I'm still a man in my prime. I've got needs. I mean look at me – why can't she see that I'm still a fine figure of a man, and any woman would be more than happy to shack up with me.'

Abruptly, the Admiral turned towards his friend so the light shone directly onto his face and leaned forward. 'Come on then man, tell me you agree.'

Jimmy took a deep breath as he dubiously regarded the watery eyes, thread veined cheeks, and larger than average nose no more than six inches in front of him

However, before he could come up with a suitably acceptable reply that wouldn't result in him standing to attention for the next four hours in front of the Admiral's dishwasher, the Admiral turned away, either indicating it was purely a rhetorical question, or he genuinely couldn't comprehend that anyone could possibly regard him as less than a prime catch.

Jimmy sighed with relief. He really hadn't got time this afternoon to do dishwasher duty as he'd agreed to take his wife shopping. Although to be fair, a four hour stint in front of an electrical appliance at the Admiral's house, with Tory sneaking him tea and biscuits, was actually preferable to four hours trailing after his wife in Marks and Spencer's. He didn't think his wife would see it that way though. Emily Noon had enough trouble understanding her husband's tolerance towards 'that dinosaur's' eccentricities as it was.

Of course, Emily wasn't aware that only the quick thinking of the dinosaur in question had, early on in their naval career, saved her husband from a potentially horrible fate involving a Thai prostitute who'd actually turned out to be a man…

As far as Jimmy was concerned, Admiral Shackleford was his Commanding Officer, and always would be, and if that involved such idiosyncrasies as presenting himself in front of a dishwasher with headphones on, saluting and saying, 'Dishwasher manned and ready sir.' Then four hours later, saluting again while saying, 'Dishwasher secured,' so be it.

It was a small price to pay... He leaned towards his morose friend and patted him on the back, showing a little manly support (acceptable, even from subordinates), while murmuring, 'Don't worry about it too much Sir. Tory's a sensible girl. She'll come round eventually – you know she wants you to be happy.' The Admiral's only response was an inelegant snort, so Jimmy ceased his patting, and went back to his pint.

Both men gazed into their drinks for a few minutes, as if all the answers would be found in the amber depths.

'What she needs is a man.' Jimmy's abrupt observation drew another rude snort, this one even louder.

'Who do you suggest? She's not interested in anyone. Says there's no one in Dartmouth she'd give house room to, and believe me I've tried. When she's not giving me grief, she spends all her time in that bloody gallery with all those airy fairy types. Can't imagine any one of them climbing her rigging. Not one set of balls between 'em.' Jimmy chuckled at the Admiral's description of Tory's testosterone challenged male friends.

'She's not ugly though,' Charles Shackleford mused, still staring into his drink. 'She might have an arse the size of an aircraft carrier, but she's got her mother's top half which balances it out nicely.'

'Aye, she's built a bit broad across the beam,' Jimmy agreed nodding his head.

'And then there's this bloody film crew. I haven't told her yet.' Jimmy frowned at the abrupt change of subject, and shot a puzzled glance over to the Admiral.

'Film crew? What film crew?'

Charles Shackleford looked back irritably. 'Come on Jimmy, get a grip. I'm talking about that group of nancies coming to film at the house next month. I must have mentioned it.'

Jimmy simply shook his head in bewilderment.

Frowning at his friend's obtuseness, the Admiral went on, 'You know, what's that bloody film they're making at the moment – big blockbuster everyone's talking about?'

'What, you mean The Bridegroom?'

'That's the one. Seems like they were looking for a large house overlooking the River Dart. Think they were hoping for Greenway, you know, Agatha Christie's place, but then they spied "the Admiralty" and said it was spot on. Paying me a packet they are. Coming next week.'

Jimmy stared at his former commanding officer with something approaching pity. 'And you've arranged all this without telling Tory?'

'None of her bloody business,' the Admiral blustered, banging his now empty pint glass on the bar, and waving at the barmaid for a refill. 'She's out most of the time anyway.'

Jimmy shook his head in disbelief. 'When are you going to tell her?'

'Was going to do it this morning, but then this business with Mabel came up so I scarpered. Last I saw she was taking that bloody little mongrel of hers out for a walk. Hoping she'll walk off her temper.' His tone indicated he considered there was more likelihood of hell freezing over.

'Is Noah Westbrook coming?' said Jimmy, suddenly sensing a bit of gossip he could pass on to Emily.

'Noah who?' was the Admiral's bewildered response.

'Noah Westbrook. Come on Sir, you must know him. He's the most famous actor in the world. Women go completely gaga over him. If nothing else, that should make Tory happy.'

The Admiral stared at him thoughtfully. 'What's he look like, this Noah West... chappy?'

The barmaid, who had been unashamedly listening to the whole conversation, couldn't contain herself any longer and, thrusting a glossy magazine under the Admiral's nose, said breathlessly, 'Like this. He looks like this.'

The full colour photograph was that of a naked man lounging on a sofa, with only a towel protecting his modesty, together with the caption "Noah Westbrook, officially voted the sexiest man on the planet."

Admiral Charles Shackleford stared pensively down at the

picture in front of him. 'So this Noah chap – he's in this film is he?'

'He's got the lead role.' The bar maid actually twittered causing the Admiral to look up in irritation – bloody woman must be fifty if she's a day. Shooting her a withering look, he went back to the magazine, and read the beginning of the article inside.

"Noah Westbrook is to be filming in the South West of England over the next month, causing a sudden flurry of bookings to hotels and guest houses in the South Devon area."

The Admiral continued to stare at the photo, the germination of an idea tiptoeing around the edges of his brain. Glancing up, he discovered he was the subject of scrutiny from not just the barmaid, but now the whole pub was waiting with bated breath to hear what he was going to say next.

The Admiral's eyes narrowed as the beginnings of a plan slowly began taking shape, but he needed to keep it under wraps. Looking around at his rapt audience, he feigned nonchalance. 'Don't think Noah Westbrook was mentioned at all in the correspondence. Think he must be filming somewhere else.'

Then, without saying anything further, he downed the rest of his drink, and climbed laboriously off his stool.

'Coming Jimmy, Pickles?' His tone was deceptively casual which fooled Jimmy not at all, and, sensing something momentous afoot, the smaller man swiftly finished his pint. In his haste to follow the Admiral out of the door, he only narrowly avoided falling over Pickles who, completely unappreciative of the need for urgency, was sitting in the middle of the floor, scratching unconcernedly behind his ear.

Once outside, the Admiral didn't bother waiting for his dog, secure in the knowledge that someone would let the elderly spaniel out before he got too far down the road. Instead, he took hold of Jimmy's arm, and dragged him out of earshot – just in case anyone was listening.

In complete contrast to his mood on arrival, Charles

Shackleford was now grinning from ear to ear. 'That's it. I've finally got a plan,' he hissed to his bewildered friend. 'I'm going to get her married off.'

'Who to?' asked Jimmy confused.

'Don't be so bloody slow Jimmy. To him of course. The actor chappy, Noah Westbrook. According to that magazine, women everywhere fall over themselves for him. Even Victory won't be able to resist him.'

Jimmy opened his mouth but nothing came out. He stared in complete disbelief as the Admiral went on. 'Then she'll move out, and Mabel can move in. Simple.'

Pickles came ambling up as Jimmy finally found his voice. 'So, let me get this straight Sir. Your plan is to somehow get Noah Westbrook, the most famous actor on the entire planet to fall in love with your daughter Victory, who we both love dearly, but - and please don't take offence Sir - who you yourself admit is built generously across the aft, and whose face is unlikely to launch the Dartmouth ferry, let alone a thousand ships.'

The Admiral frowned. 'Well admittedly, I've not worked out the finer details, but that's about the sum of it. What do you think...?'

Chapter Two

'DOTTY'

'DOTTY'

'DOTTY NOOOOO…'

Although I actually run the last few yards, I'm too late; the dirty madam has already started the roll, and is now liberally covered in fox poo.

'Bloody hell Dotty, you grubby little tart – it's in the bath for you as soon as we get home.'

I plonk her back on the lead, trying as far as possible to avoid the big lump of fox doo that is now clumped around her muzzle.

'You are so disgusting.' I mutter, dragging her along the path.

Dotty is a Bichon Frise crossed with a Chihuahua (the breeder called her a Chi-Chon, which I think might be another word for mongrel with a high price tag.) She has fur resembling nylon, and a disturbing tendency to roll in anything she finds that's even slightly revolting. She is also the love of my life. Most of the time.

I had intended to walk the trail all the way to Dittisham, in an attempt to walk off my current frustration towards my unpredictable, idiosyncratic, and only surviving parent. However, the ghastly smell rising from my badly behaved mutt who is looking far too pleased with herself, has put paid to that, and I decide to head back straight to the Admiralty. The name of our house is only one of many eccentricities of my father. Names have always been a bit of a thing for him – starting with mine.

Which happens to be Victory Britannia Shackleford, after his two favourite ships in the Battle of Trafalgar...

I've never really forgiven him. Luckily, the only one who actually calls me Victory is my father. Everyone else shortens it to Tory, for which I am profoundly grateful.

Carefully keeping Dotty downwind, I begin the descent through the woods towards the house. It's early May, and the bluebells carpet the forest floor in a sea of royal blue. As I walk, I keep catching glimpses of the Dart Estuary through the trees. The sunlight sparkling on the water is almost otherworldly, and only the distant sound of the car ferry crossing over to the picturesque town of Dartmouth on the other side of the river, reminds me that Dotty and I aren't completely alone.

I love moments like these, and taking a deep breath, I slowly feel my anger subside. I know I'm being unreasonable. My father is perfectly entitled to a relationship, and it isn't like he's cheating on mum – she's been dead for over six years.

Picking my way carefully down the steep track, I finally admit to myself that my anger is more out of fear. If he has another woman, dad won't need me anymore. I'll have to move out. Leave the only home I've ever known. Panic grips me at the mere thought, and I feel my anger turn inwards. It's just bloody ridiculous. Nearly thirty three years old, and still living with my father. It's not like I can't afford to get a place of my own. My interior design business is doing well, and mum left me well provided for.

It isn't about money. I simply can't bear the thought of losing my only surviving parent. Six years down the line, the pain of my mum's death is still as fresh as if it was yesterday. While I'm living at home, I can stop anything like that ever happening again. I can ensure that nothing bad happens to my madcap, reckless, not to mention completely irresponsible father. Just like mum did.

I give a deep sigh. The problem is, I'm not my mum. I know dad loves me, but this morning I realized for the first time that maybe he doesn't actually like me very much. I cringe as I recall his actual words earlier. 'I hate to say it Victory, but you've turned into a boring, nagging harpy with no imagination, or sense of adventure.'

Maybe he's right. Maybe it is time I began to see life more like he does. As I finally break free of the trees, and climb down the few overgrown steps to the road, I decide to speak with dad again at dinner. I am determined to prove to him that there is more to me than a repetitive nag. I am fully capable of living life on the edge, and signing up to his philosophy of "living for today".

As I start down the road towards the house, I feel a pull on the lead and glance down at Dotty who is finally getting over the doggie euphoria of disguising her scent with one resembling a dead skunk. No doubt picturing the all too familiar tin bath tub that's waiting for her in the garage.

Deep in thought, I don't notice until I'm almost at the gate that a small crowd has gathered on the grass verge, pushing and shoving in an effort to peer down into the gardens surrounding the Admiralty.

Our house is a beautiful Edwardian manor built at the turn of the century to take full advantage of the glorious River Dart. On the other side is The Britannia Royal Naval College where all Royal Navy Officer Training takes place. The Admiralty was originally owned by one of the earliest Commodores in charge of the place. It was ideally situated to keep an eye on any shenanigans going on in the College. As another ex-commodore listed in its hallowed halls, this is a pastime my father still engages in with total enthusiasm, aided by an up to the minute set of binoculars.

I really do love my father, but how he ever got promoted to Admiral will forever remain a mystery, not least I suspect to the Royal Navy. When asked, he usually mumbles something about being in the wrong place at the wrong time...

The Admiralty's extensive grounds slope down towards the river and the higher car ferry, giving a beautiful open vista of the bend in the river as it snakes away in the direction of Totnes towards the right, and the sea towards the left.

It's usually very quiet and private, and the crowd are struggling to see anything through the fence, so I wander up to ask what all the commotion is.

'Is he here?'

'When are they starting filming?'

'God, I'm so envious.'

'You must be so nervous Tory.'

'I'm from the Herald Express...'

In seconds I'm surrounded. What the hell is going on? Not one to enjoy crowds, Dotty is standing practically on top of me, and trying very hard to jump in to my arms (which would be lovely in normal circumstances...)

I'm tempted to shout 'QUIET,' in an effort to stop the verbal onslaught coming at me from every direction. In the end however, Eau de Dotty wins out...

'Oh my God, what the hell is that horrible smell?' comes from the person nearest me, and slowly the crowd start to back off as I vainly protest that it isn't me... Just when I decide that the whole of Dartmouth and Kingswear have gone mad, I spot my best friend Kit fighting her way through from the back of the throng.

'Oh my God you stink,' she states without preamble.

'Not me,' I say for what seems like the hundredth time, and point down to my errant pooch, who is now trying to rub what remains of the fox poo on my trousers.

'What on earth's going on Kitty Kat – do you know?'

Kit has been my best friend since primary school. She is the ying to my yang, blond to my dark, tall and willowy to my, er, "womanly" curves, drop dead gorgeous to my "homeliness" – and above all, oozing confidence to my less than sparkling personality...

She's responsible for every scrape I've ever gotten into throughout my whole life, and I love her dearly. At the moment Kit is peering at me in slight disbelief. Then, shaking her head in resignation, 'Why am I surprised you don't know?'

I simply stare at her impatiently, knowing her flair for the dramatic. She didn't disappoint. 'You, my introverted, sensible, occasionally boring, never melodramatic, BFF, are about to have your humdrum, orderly existence turned completely upside down – at least for the next few weeks anyway…'

I frown and attempt to interrupt, but she forestalls me by holding up her hand, and for the first time I can see her pent up excitement, and feel an answering tug in the pit of my stomach. I can tell she's about to deliver the punch line, and is loving every minute.

'Only the most famous, gorgeous, sexiest, richest actor on the entire planet is going to be filming in Dartmouth and... most probably in your house.'

I frown, and look around at the crowd still hovering across the road. 'What the bloody hell are you talking about?'

Grasping my arms tightly, Kit stares intently into my face. 'Noah Westbrook. THE Noah Westbrook. Is. Coming. To. Film. In. Your. House.'

'Don't be ridiculous. Why on earth would Noah Westbrook want to film our house?'

Kit sighs again, this time in frustration. 'He's not filming your house. He's filming IN your house.'

I open my mouth with the intention of scoffing again. Then I pause, looking at my finally silent friend. Surely Dad would have told me. He couldn't possibly have kept something as monumental as this a secret – could he? 'How do you know all this?'

'Bumped into the barmaid from the Ship in Kingswear. Apparently your father let it slip to the whole pub.'

I think back to the last few weeks. The furtive telephone calls, the long periods closeted in his study – all of which I'd put down to his clandestine affair with the merry widow. My heart starts to beat faster, and Kit can see the acceptance in my face.

'Oh shit, Kit. This time he's gone too far. I really will kill him. When are they coming – do you know?' Before she can answer, the crowd begin to surge forward again, and I turn round in time to see the object of my murderous fantasies walking towards the house with Pickles at his heels. I think he was trying to sneak in with no-one noticing. One look at my face however tells him there's no chance of that.

Dotty, completely oblivious to the undercurrents, gives a joyful bark, and bounds up to Pickles who appears to love the scent of Eau de Fox Poo, and sniffs around her appreciatively, wagging his tail. Dotty simply wags her own tail back, and holds still to give him maximum access...

The crowd jostle to get as close to the Admiral as possible, all the while firing questions at him about the most exciting celebrity news to hit Dartmouth since the Pilgrim Fathers sailed off to found America nearly four hundred years ago...

Glancing towards me, the traitorous, lying toad coughs and waves his hand before shouting over the din. 'Bloody hell, give a fellow a chance to breathe. Noah Westbrook is NOT coming here. No idea where he's going. They're just filming the bit parts in the Admiralty gardens, that's all, and it's only for a couple of weeks.'

With that, and an additional – admittedly apprehensive – glance my way, he pushes open the gate and disappears, Pickles and Dotty at his heels, before the crowd can question him further.

I glance over at Kit, who is looking pretty disappointed, and I can understand why. Her visions of being whisked off her feet by the world's most popular actor have been trampled into the dust. To be fair, if I'm being honest, I'm feeling a slight pang of regret at my father's words, (which just goes to show that I'm not *always* sensible, and maybe even enjoy the occasional melodrama – there's hope for me yet...) I simply give her a quick hug, and promise to keep her posted, before hurrying after my father. As I shut the gate, the thwarted crowd begins to dissipate behind me, and I breathe a sigh of relief.

~*~

'I've told you a dozen times - I was supposed to keep shtum about it Victory. Don't you think I'd have told you if I could have?' I glare sceptically at my father's innocent face. His tone has turned suspiciously wheedling – always a sign that he's lying through his teeth. Realizing that I have absolutely no chance of getting to the complete truth of the matter, I reluctantly hand in the towel. Besides, the extra money from the film crew will enable us to do some of the much needed repairs to the mausoleum we live in.

'Well at least we haven't got to worry about the paparazzi hiding in the bushes trying to get a shot of the world's most famous actor having a cup of tea in our kitchen,' I mutter as Dottie's barking reaches a crescendo outside – she's been left literally in the dog house to contemplate the error of her ways, before being subject to the dreaded bath.

However, before I get out of the room, my father's words stop me in my tracks. 'Ah well, might have been slightly off the mark there...' I feel a dull thud in my chest, and my heart begins to beat rapidly. I turn round, and wait for my father to drop the bombshell I know is coming...

I notice for the first time that he's holding a piece of paper in his hand, which he waves towards me as he hurriedly continues, 'Had another look at the letter, and it does happen to mention Noah what's-his-face will be part of the crew filming here. In fact it actually says he's already in Dartmouth.... incognito, so to speak.'

I turn round slowly to look at my father, who is now grinning in triumph like some demented Cheshire cat, and resist the urge to throttle him with my bare hands. 'What do you mean, he's already in Dartmouth? Where is he staying?' I'm amazed at how calm my voice sounds.

Dad must have sensed something in my voice, because his smile falters a bit as he continues, 'Well, not *in* Dartmouth exactly. He's on this side of the river, in Kingswear. Think he's renting a house up on the cliffs. They've even given me his temporary mobile phone number. Thought we might invite him for dinner tomorrow night if he's free – let him get the feel of the place, soak in the atmosphere... You know what these

actor types are like; bit of a thespian thing.
'What do you think...?'

Friday 2nd May

To: kim@kimharris.com

Hey sis how's things in sunny California? Ben and the kids ok?

Weather in England not living up to its rep - since I've been here we've had sun every day. Kinda nice actually – not as hot as home but love the light, especially first thing in the morning when the mist sits just on top of the River Dart waiting for the sun to burn through it – would you believe I'm getting the urge to paint – where the hell did that come from? I've settled in to my rental. You'd love it, great house with fantastic views over the river and out to sea. It's in a little place called Kingswear on the other side of the River, facing Dartmouth – which by the way is a great town – really quaint and you know, British. I've had a few days to explore under cover without looking a complete goof wearing sun glasses in the pouring rain.

I've not seen the house we're filming in yet, but actually been asked round for dinner by the owner, a guy by the name of Charles Shackleford. Seems he's a retired Admiral. Lives with his daughter, who he spent the whole time assuring me 'scrubs up well', and is more than capable of putting together a nice bit of 'scran', whatever the hell that means. He sounds a bit of a kook, and she probably looks like Nanny McFee (hopefully without the warts...)

Anyway, couldn't come up with a good excuse, and it was obvious the old guy wasn't gonna take no for an answer, so would you believe I'm walking over tomorrow evening for supper – least I'm hoping that's what 'scran' means :-)

Long time since I've been anywhere without a posse. Guess I really needed the space. Might even be fun. Will keep you posted.

Anyway Kimmy, I'm zonked – can't remember the last time I had so much fresh air. It'll be the death of me.

Give the kids a kiss from me

Noah xxx

Chapter Three

As the Friday evening weather continued with its unseasonable warmth, Admiral Shackleford decided to take his first pint out on to the terrace. Jimmy, who of course had no say in the matter, loyally followed him out into the sunshine. They sat side by side in companionable silence for a few minutes, while Pickles busied himself trying to catch flies.

After about fifteen minutes, Jimmy could contain himself no longer, and brought up their lunchtime conversation. 'So, how's the plan going Sir?' he asked breathlessly. 'Have you spoken to Tory yet? Does she know about Noah Westbrook? How are you going to get them together?' As the barrage of questions came to an end, the Admiral glanced down at his friend in annoyance before saying, 'What the hell's wrong with you Jimmy, you had a brain fart? Someone might be ear wigging. Better check the perimeter before we get down to business.' Jimmy glanced around apologetically, fully expecting to see the half a dozen regulars with their ears plastered to the door. Fortunately, the coast appeared to be clear, and Jimmy breathed a sigh of relief, and gave the Admiral the thumbs up sign.

The Admiral cleared his throat, looked once behind him, and turned to face his friend before whispering triumphantly, 'I have been in contact with the package. Turns out he's already in Kingswear, and has agreed to come round for dinner. Tomorrow night.'

'Blimey Sir, that was quick work. Very impressive Sir, very impressive indeed.' The Admiral waved away his friend's admiration and leaned back in his chair, a picture of total self satisfaction at a mission going according to plan.

'Does Tory know?' The self satisfied smirk slipped a notch at Jimmy's continued probing. 'Of course she knows,' he answered irritably, 'told her this afternoon. She knows the package has already been delivered to the area, as it were.' The Admiral paused before continuing, 'She thought it was a top notch idea to invite the package to dinner.'

Jimmy nodded his head in admiring agreement as he pondered the Admiral's bold and cunning plan. That was Admiral Shackleford. Always lived life on the edge, never afraid to make tough decisions and take chances. What a man. Jimmy took a long draft of his pint...

'Thought I'd ask Mabel Pomfrey to make up a foursome.'

...And promptly spat it out all over Pickles head.

Chapter Four

'So, is he coming...?' Kit's near shout stops me in mid "woe is me" and causes Dotty to take up the mantle in furious excited barking.

'Now look what you've done,' I answer irritably, grabbing the little dog before she decides to launch herself off Kit's balcony window.

We're sitting in her tiny but cosy flat in the centre of Dartmouth where I've been doing my best to work through a bottle of wine since arriving an hour ago. 'I've no idea, I walked out of the house before I ended up committing patricide.'

My best friend sags back into her chair with a disappointed thump and I bury my face in my now sweet smelling little mutt who begins licking my nose enthusiastically.

'I just can't understand you Tory. You must be absolutely the only woman in the whole world who is not moved to squealing delirium at the thought of spending an evening with the biggest heartthrob on the planet. What the hell's wrong with you? How many women do you think would literally commit murder to be in your shoes right now?'

'Yeah well, they haven't got a father like mine,' I respond sourly, plonking Dotty back down in my lap, 'and three's definitely a crowd, especially when the third one is just as likely to stand on the piano and give a rousing rendition of "What Shall We Do With The Drunken Sailor" after he's had a couple of glasses of port.

'He's going to think we're absolutely barking Kit, I know he is.

And I haven't got the looks or the wit to offset any negative first impressions.' Unexpectedly I feel tears gathering in the corner of my eyes and I swallow convulsively and bury my head in Dotty's warm little body again in an effort to stem a possible flood.

Kit stays tactfully silent, concern evident in her eyes and waits for me to regain my composure. She knows me all too well and recognizes that this behaviour just isn't me. I'm the practical one who has an answer or a solution to everything. I *never* fall apart...

After a couple of minutes I look up and give her a watery smile. 'I'm sure he won't come anyway. Like you said, he's a big name actor with legions of adoring fans. Why on earth would he want to spend a Saturday evening with an eccentric sailor and a dried up old spinster?'

'Is that it? Have you finished the pity party now?' Kit's words and tone are not quite as soothingly sympathetic as I think the situation warrants, but before I get the chance to open my mouth with a suitably indignant retort, she holds up her hand and continues, 'I'll grant you that the Admiral is more often than not a sandwich short of a picnic, but you have to admit he's never boring, especially at a dinner party.

'And you, a dried up old spinster? I don't think so. It wasn't a dried up old spinster who organized a flash mob involving half of Dartmouth for Freddy's thirtieth birthday two years ago, or climbed the rigging for a bet on Ben Sheppard's yacht last summer or took part in the Boxing Day Swimathon in Torquay last Christmas dressed as a donkey... Sensible you may be – when you have to, but dried up, most definitely not. And you're only in your thirties for God's sake. I'm sure you're not allowed to be a dried up anything until you're at least sixty.'

Against my will I feel myself blushing and laugh ruefully. Leaning forward, I raise my glass to her in defeat. 'Okay smart arse, so, if you've got all the answers, what shall I wear to this sparkling dinner party that states witty, intelligent, attractive, fascinating, alluring, charming, charismatic woman of the world in her prime?

'And not only that, what the hell am I going to cook...?' It's not often I see Kit lost for words.

An hour later I'm wobbling down Fore Street towards the higher ferry with Dotty at my heels. Since my dearest friend is approximately three sizes smaller than my generous curves (her words - if I remember right, I used the word buxom, probably as a result of reading too many bodice rippers), it was out of the question that I borrow a knock 'em dead outfit from her wardrobe. Which meant of course we had to crack open another bottle of wine while dissecting my admittedly meagre and eclectic (my words – if I remember right, she favoured measly, paltry, inadequate and frumpy) mix of clothes. The general consensus was that I need a new dress...

I really don't know why we're going to all this trouble, it's not like he's going to fall in love with me for God's sake!

Anyway, I'm not too inebriated to know that clothes shopping while feeling slightly worse for wear is not a good idea for two reasons: Firstly, I can't see the mirror properly and secondly, what I do see will unfortunately be way better than reality (or when I'm sober).

So, after much hugging, kissing and protestations of undying friendship and love, Kit and I decide to reconvene tomorrow first thing when we will begin the daunting task of creating a whole new sexy me...

And the food? Of course that will necessitate a visit to Marks and Spencer's Gastropub selection. All this and I don't even know if he's actually coming yet.

I decide to walk along the promenade towards the higher car ferry which will get me home the quickest. (The Admiralty gardens meander down to the water's edge, right next to the ferry slip on the other side of the river where there is a very useful gate to the road.) I still have enough sense to know that the most direct route will probably be the wisest at this moment in time given that I definitely need a lie down.

There are actually two car ferries going to and fro across the river Dart – the Higher and Lower. The advantage of the Higher one, (obviously depending on where you want to go), is that it puts passengers off higher up the River. It's much larger than the lower one and passes for what could be described in the west country as "high powered" (actually taking thirty two cars at a time...) The Lower Ferry takes passengers directly over to the small village of Kingswear which faces Dartmouth across the river. It only takes about eight cars at a time and is about as far from high powered as you can get without actually rowing. The blurb describes it as "historical". I think archaic might be a better word. Not so long ago, it broke from its mooring and only the quick thinking ferrymen prevented the passengers potentially disembarking in France.

There's also a passenger ferry and we Dartmothians residing on the dark side (as we call the other side of the river) tend to juggle between the three modes of transport depending on the time of day, the weather and level of inebriation. Rowing yourself across is also an option but usually only done in times of dire emergency and no ferries – for example, three o'clock in the morning.

As it's still only early evening, no such drastic measures are necessary; for which I'm sure Dotty at least is profoundly grateful.

As I arrive at the Higher Ferry Slip, I note that said ferry is right over the other side and decide to have a much needed rest on one of the benches outside the Floating Bridge pub which very handily is right next to the ferry queue. I can't help but notice a guy sitting on the bench opposite with sunglasses on (it really isn't that sunny), reading a book as he sips a pint of beer and dips into a basket of French fries. The smell is heavenly and reminds me that I haven't actually eaten anything substantial since this morning. He looks vaguely familiar and I glance surreptitiously at him as I sit, trying to think where I've seen him before.

While my interest is discreet, Dotty has no such qualms and

is now straining on the leash to get closer to the source of the delicious smell, all the while wagging her tail furiously. Before I realise it, she has launched herself up onto the stranger's knee. She really is such a tart...

Startled, the man nearly chokes on his pint, but to his credit he doesn't simply shove Dotty off but smiles down at her and gives her a French fry, thus earning her undying love forever.

All this happens in a nanosecond - my dog is nothing if not an opportunist - and I jump up as quickly as my unsteady state will allow, mumbling my embarrassed apologies (when did I start slurring?)

As I lurch forward, I drop Dotty's leash and grab her from the stranger's arms... who is now looking up at me with his eyebrows slightly raised. (Oh God he knows I'm squiffy, mortified doesn't even begin to cut it – it's only six o'clock in the evening for pity's sake...)

I continue to mutter rambling requests for forgiveness while trying to admonish my delinquent mutt at the same time. My face is now the colour of a ripe tomato and I turn hurriedly with the intent of spending the rest of my wait as far away from the man as possible. Unfortunately my feet have other ideas as I step into the handle of the leash. Dotty yelps loudly as the force of my foot yanks her upside down and I'm briefly left holding on to her bottom before I let her go and stumble forward, all the while trying to get my foot out of the leash handle. Seconds later I am sprawled face down on the concrete where I remain for a couple of seconds, slightly stunned.

Then humiliation sets in. I can hear the stranger jump up behind me (damn it, he can see my backside – must look massive from his direction; why oh why did I change my jeans? Which knickers am I wearing...?) I debate briefly whether I should go for broke and pretend a broken ankle (or at the very least a sprained one). Dotty is now licking the side of my face furiously and I can feel the presence of the man as he crouches to my other side. Where's a deep dark hole when you need one...

As I groan slightly (got to give it at least some theatrics) and lift my head, I catch a glimpse of the ferry arriving at the slip and decide to cut and run (my acting skills really are not that good...)

I jump up, nearly head butting the stranger in the process who fortunately reels back just in time to save what could have been a broken nose, grab Dotty's leash and take off in a sprint that could have given Mo Farah a run for his money.

Dodging the boarding cars, I continue my headlong dash down the ferry slipway without looking back at my would be rescuer. I don't stop until I'm under cover in the designated foot passenger area where I can no longer see the Floating Bridge, which means the stranger can no longer see me. Groaning and wheezing, I lean my head against the wall, feeling the vibration of the engines as the ferry begins its crossing. The groaning is of course my response to my recent total and abject humiliation, pure and simple. The wheezing part? Well, I don't do running. In fact under normal circumstances, if you see me running, it's a strong indication that you should probably run too, because the chances are that something nasty is chasing me...

As my mind replays the horror of the last fifteen minutes in a continuous loop, I can actually feel myself sobering up until my attention is brought back to the present by a small whimper coming from my feet. I look down to see Dotty plastered to the deck – all four paws splayed out in abject terror and my heart goes out to her. I'd forgotten how much she hates the car ferry. I think it's the feel of the engines rumbling away under her feet. Bending down I pick her up into my arms and snuggle her into my neck where she gratefully burrows. I determine to put the whole sorry incident right out of my mind and just thank my lucky stars that I'm never likely to see the man again.

Although it would've been nice to have seen what he looked like without the sunglasses.

What seems like three hours later - but is really only about twenty minutes - I arrive puffing and panting at the house. Did I mention that the Admiralty's gardens stretch right down to the river? Well that's all fine and dandy - however, the downside is that half of it is at a forty five degree angle. God knows why they want to use it for a movie.

As I push open the back door and step into the dim interior, Dotty's barked greeting is answered by Pickles, indicating that my father's at home. Rightly assuming he's hiding in his study, which is where Pickles' muffled barking is coming from, I knock hard on the door.

The interior of the Admiralty is a testament to a bygone age. Oak panelling, hardwood floors, galleried landing, large open fireplaces, and tributes everywhere to British naval history. I defy anyone remotely patriotic to walk into this house without feeling an insane urge to burst into the first verse of "Land of Hope and Glory". It's certainly not to everyone's taste. But definitely to Hollywood's it seems...

Dad is doing his best to ignore my knocks. However, the crescendo coming from the two dogs is making it impossible for even him to disregard and eventually he opens the door. 'So, is he coming?' I ask without preamble.

'Now I know it's all a bit much for you Tory,' he responds without actually answering my question. *And* he called me Tory; always a very bad sign. I feel a headache coming on that has nothing to do with my hangover. 'I really want you to relax and enjoy yourself tomorrow evening...'

'So he *is* coming,' I interrupt - the headache is now warring with a sick feeling in the pit of my stomach.

'Well, err yes, said he'd be pleased to attend – pretty polite actually for a Yank. Anyway, thought I'd do you a favour and get somebody else to help you with the cooking and, you know, make up a foursome like'

The headache and the sick feeling is now joined by a shortness of breath. Think I might be having a heart attack... 'Who?' I manage to whisper.

'Asked Mabel. Thought it'd be a cracking opportunity for you to get to know each other.'

Chapter Five

It's six thirty in the evening and I think I've finally got everything under control. I feel like I've been up for twenty hours, (actually I probably have given that I didn't sleep a wink last night), and after a totally manic day, I'm absolutely knackered.

After informing my idiot father this morning, (I was completely incapable of saying anything last night that didn't end up with my hands around his neck – beginning to think I might need to undergo anger management therapy), that under no circumstances did I want Mabel Pomfrey anywhere near my kitchen, even if it's soon to be hers, Kit and I raided Marks and Spencer's, so at least I'm fairly confident that I'm unlikely to poison anybody.

We have dipping breads to start, pasta for the main course and cheesecake for dessert – what can go wrong with that?

So now, here I am, hair brushed and gleaming, as much as my wayward curls will allow, make up subtle (which of course took half a bottle of foundation), and all that's left is for me to put on my new dress which was Kit's choice and I'm not at all sure about.

Fitted into the waist, the dress is navy and white. Kit said I looked like a young Sophia Loren when I tried it on - but she wasn't wearing her glasses at the time.

Looking at myself now, I'm beginning to panic a bit and wonder if I should chicken out and wear my old trusty floral sack (Kit's words). But what the hell does it matter anyway. At least I don't look dowdy and spinsterish. So Sophia Loren it is. Maybe Noah Westbrook wears glasses. Let the fun begin...

Unfortunately it appears that Mabel has arrived early, the clue being the muted giggling coming from the living room. It's going to be a long night.

I throw open the door as loudly as I can and let Dotty do her thing while I head directly to the kitchen. Instantly the muted giggling turns to shrieks and I can't help but smile to myself, especially as I know that Pickles will have wasted no time in turning it into a cosy foursome on the sofa. That's my girl...

Twenty minutes later and I know I can't loiter in the kitchen any longer. Everything is ready to go. I'm already half way into my first glass of wine and the only thing worse than being introduced to Mabel Pomfrey is being introduced to her in front of the most famous actor in the world whilst trollied. So I top up my glass and reluctantly head over to the living room.

As I enter the room, Dotty jumps off the sofa in sheer joy at seeing me and I just have time to note that she has spent the entire time sandwiched between my father and his paramour before my father jumps up, more flustered than I've ever seen him, to make the introductions.

As he fusses, holding out a hand to help Mabel to her feet, I feel a surge of love for him that surprises me. It's not often that my irascible parent is out of his depth, but it's suddenly clear that this meeting is actually very important to him and I resolve in that instant to do my best to make it easy for him.

As Mabel struggles to her feet, I place my wine glass on the coffee table and, moving forward, plaster a smile to my face and hold out my hand. Unfortunately, Mabel is having none of it and surges forward to clasp me into her ample bosom before planting a resounding (and very wet) kiss onto each of my cheeks. Then she holds each of my arms while gushing enthusiastically about our forthcoming intimate relations.

I don't really have an answer to this except to hope profusely that by relations, she actually means relationship. I spend the next few seconds staring in morbid fascination at two very hairy moles decorating her top lip and chin, while I struggle for something to say. I can see my father out of the corner of my eye grinning from ear to ear and I feel like I'm in the middle of a horror movie.

And then the doorbell rings... Of course Dotty goes berserk and dashes to the front door, her barking reaching an ear splitting climax, to which Pickles then adds his enthusiastic howls.

I hurriedly extricate myself from Mabel's fervent embrace and rush into the hall in an effort to quieten the dogs down. Unfortunately my father's yelling behind me to 'Shut those bloody dogs up' is doing nothing to help the situation. Which I'm sure can't possibly get any worse.

Dragging Dotty and Pickles out of the way, I fling open the door and stare in total horror at the stranger from the Floating Bridge. This time without his sunglasses.

I'm hiding in the kitchen. I've been here for five minutes forty eight seconds under the pretext of getting drinks and nibbles. However, instead of being the gracious hostess, I am rocking back and forth in my chair while chewing the ends of my finger nails. Dotty is sat at my feet looking up at me with her head cocked to the side. She whines softly, sensing my distress. Pickles has been consigned to the study.

I know I have to go out there, but I just can't seem to make my feet move. My mind keeps playing back the last ten minutes in full Technicolor...

When I finally opened the door, Dotty threw herself at the man standing there as if they were long lost friends (she has a long memory where food is concerned). I remember him stepping back laughing while holding his gift of a bottle of wine over his head, then bending down to stroke her head gently, before looking up at me standing there like a complete loon.

'Hello again,' he murmured softly, the smile still in his eyes. And oh my God those eyes...

Pure blue, heavy lidded, and framed by long black lashes that most women would kill for.

Then he stood back up. He was tall, easily a good six inches over my five foot seven, lean with broad shoulders. His hair, worn slightly longer in defiance of current fashion, fell across his forehead in thick waves, so black, it was almost blue, with just a smattering of grey at the temples.

With dark bronzed skin, generous mouth, and slightly arrogant jaw, he was quite simply the most beautiful man I had ever seen.

And what did I do? I waved him in, snatched the bottle out of his hand, mumbled 'wine' three times, and fled back to the kitchen.

It's now seven minutes and twenty four seconds. There are no sounds coming from the living room where I assume our guest has been taken and I wonder if I can make it to the front door without anyone seeing me. I actually stand up and take a step forward in preparation for my escape when the living room door opens and out stomps my father.

'What the bloody hell are you doing Victory?' he shouts. I close my eyes with a moan and sink back into the chair, just as he throws open the kitchen door. 'Come on girl,' he continues in his best booming voice, 'get your arse in gear, it's like the bloody Sahara Desert in there. Where's the wets?'

I look up with the intention of telling him exactly what he can do with his wets, when I suddenly realize that Noah Westbrook has been left in the living room with Mabel Pomfrey... As the significance of this sinks in, self pity is replaced by a sudden certainty of impending doom. This could go national, or even international. Oh. My. God.

I jump up so quickly that Dotty falls over in surprise. Without speaking, I thrust the crisps and nibbles into my father's startled hands, then, after pushing him towards the kitchen door, I turn back to the table and quickly uncork the wine. Reasoning that if he brought red, he must like red, I slosh the contents of the bottle into four glasses and plonk them on a tray.

Turning round I see that dad is still standing there staring at me. 'What are you doing?' I hiss waving the tray towards him and only narrowly avoiding tipping its contents over Dotty's head. 'Get out there, NOW…'

Hastily my father does as I ask (definitely a first) and I follow hard on his heels. As we cross the hall, I can hear Mabel simpering (no other word for it) in the living room. 'I do so love your films,' she is gushing, 'especially Dysentried, so exciting…'

I shove my father unceremoniously through the door in time to see our famous guest frowning slightly as he tries to come up with a reply that won't offend. Mabel is now tittering. I just want a hole to swallow me up.

'The name of the film is Disoriented', I announce loudly, 'It's a movie about a man who doesn't know where he is, not one who has an infectious disease.' I know my declaration is unkind as well as unnecessary, adding guilt to my growing plethora of emotions as Mabel subsides into embarrassed silence.

I place the drinks tray on the coffee table as the silence lengthens and note, without actually looking, that Noah Westbrook is seated alone on the sofa. On the right hand end. I groan inwardly. I can't sit on the other sofa with my father and Mabel. The silence is now deafening.

I look frantically towards my father, frowning at him to introduce me. He clears his throat obligingly before saying formally, 'This my daughter Victory. She's thirty two, still lives at home and her job is err, well err, I reckon she pretty much titivates people's houses for a living.'

Oh my God, can it get any worse? I now sound like a DIY woman of the night…

Picking up the first wine glass, and, resisting the temptation to down it in one, I take a deep breath, wondering how the hell I'm going to rescue the situation. I really need to get a grip. Turning towards Mabel, I hand her the glass and mouth an apology for my rudeness, then, unable to put it off any longer, I hand the next glass to our guest. I know I can't look at the floor for the rest of the evening so I take a chance and raise my eyes to his as he murmurs his thanks.

Unbelievably there is a twinkle in his eyes and I can see that, far from being uncomfortable, he appears to actually be enjoying all the melodrama. I don't know whether to smile at him or sit down and cry. I opt for handing him the bowl of nibbles instead and Dottie comes to my rescue in her never-ending search for the ultimate snack by choosing that moment to jump up onto his lap.

Fortunately, as our earlier encounter suggested, he really does seem to like dogs, and smiling, he turns his attention to the greedy little madam perched on his knee. Ridiculously grateful for the interruption, I grab a glass of wine for myself, (I've now got two on the go – the other is still sitting on the coffee table), and taking a huge gulp, sit gingerly on the other end of the sofa.

The only noise in the room is the sound of Dotty as she chomps on a particularly large nacho. The Admiral clears his throat to speak and I quickly knock back the rest of the glass in nervous anticipation of my father's variation on small talk. 'So, er, Noah – can I call you Noah?' He politely pauses to wait for the actor's consent before continuing (he did spend nearly forty years in the Royal Navy and knows how to do cultured and refined *when* he wants to – which is rarely...)

On receiving the go-ahead, he continues in his loudest and most jovial voice. 'Must be nice to be the object of so many womanly fantasies *Noah*. Why, I'm sure even our hard to please Victory here – who I must say is the most picky female on the planet - has most likely got the hots for you...'

I'm going to kill him...

'I mean to say she's got no time for the lily livered specimens here in Dartmouth – in fact I'll be honest with you and say that I was wondering at one time if she was batting for the other side.

Slowly and with great relish...

'But I think it's safe to say, she's a red blooded lass and no mistake.' He actually pauses at that point as if awaiting confirmation from Noah Westbrook who is simply staring at him - possibly in total disbelief. Mabel is nodding her head sagely as if my father has just delivered a piece of divine wisdom.

Gritting my teeth (it's not like I'm unused to my father's gaffes when in polite company), I make an effort to laugh lightly. 'Oh dad, you're such a tease,' I chuckle, all the while glaring murderously at him behind my now sadly empty wine glass (Can I grab the extra one without anyone noticing?) 'Please don't embarrass our guest – he doesn't know you well enough to understand your little jokes.'

I turn towards our now bemused visitor and continue brightly, 'Pay no attention to my father. He simply can't resist pulling someone's leg when the opportunity arises. And anyway, it's time for dinner.' I stand up and actually clap my hands a la Mary Poppins. Fortunately I manage to resist bursting into a rendition of 'A spoon full of sugar,' in true Julie Andrews' style, thus sealing our reputation as Dartmouth's answer to the Adams Family.

There is no way I'm leaving Noah Westbrook alone in my father's company for a second longer. Fortunately the bread and dips are already waiting on the dining room table so I smile sweetly down at him while holding my hand out in invitation towards the dining room (my other hand is clutching the second glass of wine which I managed to snatch in a cunning sleight of hand that would have confounded Houdini).

'Would you like to follow me?' Unfortunately I'm almost undone when he stands up. He is so close, the slight aroma of his cologne drifts towards my nose and unable to help myself, I sway towards him - only to catch a glimpse of my father's self satisfied grin over the actor's shoulder. Unbelievably, he's winking and nodding his head up and down, and I frown as my internal alarm bells start ringing immediately.

What the hell is the old bugger up to? Abruptly I step away, putting as much distance between me and temptation (not to mention most definite humiliation) as possible. Taking a deep breath, I lead the way into the dining room. Although it's still early evening and light outside, there are lighted candles on the round dining table and in the sconces on the wall, giving the room a cosy intimate glow. My apprehension rises another notch and we haven't even eaten yet...

As my father tops up everybody's wine, I hurriedly sit down opposite our guest (can't bring myself to call him Noah), reasoning that the further away I am, the less likely I am to make a complete tit of myself (without dad's help anyway). However, as I hand over the basket of bread, I can't help but stare. His fingers touch mine as he takes the basket with a murmured thank you and my face flames as if he's just said 'I love you.' What the hell is wrong with me? I take another gulp of wine. I notice that I'm not the only one who's star struck. Dotty is lying next to his chair gazing up at him adoringly (she's not even whining for food) and Mabel is just sitting with a silly grin on her face (immunity doesn't come with age obviously).

The conversation is nonexistent. After a couple of minutes with the only sounds coming from the dipping and chewing of bread and Mabel's false teeth, I'm actually praying that my father will say something, anything – I don't care what – nothing could be worse than this awful silence...

'Tell me about your beautiful house. It obviously has a lot of history and I'd love to get a feel for the place before all my movie buddies descend on it.'

And in a flash, the conversation starts up again. It doesn't take much to get my father started on the ins and outs of his beloved Admiralty, and unknowingly our visitor had hit on exactly the right subject. I breathe a sigh of relief and relax slightly, secure in the knowledge that we're on pretty safe ground – for the time being anyway. I get up and head towards the kitchen with the intention of bringing in the pasta.

As I cross the hall, I stumble slightly on hearing dad begin his anecdote about the commodore and his parrot but luckily the response is a hearty laugh...

Amazingly the evening has not been a complete and utter disaster. Once my father realized that Noah (obviously some of my inhibitions had disappeared by the fourth glass of wine) enjoyed British humour, he kept the anecdotes coming thick and fast and although some were most definitely a bit risqué, I'd actually forgotten what a good host the Admiral could be when on top form.

It's now after midnight and Mabel is snoring softly in the corner. I've been content to sit and listen for the last hour as both men trade increasingly far-fetched naval stories for equally implausible Hollywood ones. Turns out Noah Westbrook has wit and charm as well as looks. It's a shame, I would have felt so much better had he been an arrogant twit, but alas, against my will, I am charmed like the rest of the world.

As the clock chimes half past the hour, our guest glances at his watch and murmurs that it's time he was getting back as the walk is likely to take him a good hour. 'Walk?' my father booms, rousing Mabel from her nap. 'Can't possibly risk you falling into the river at this time of night.' (As though falling in at any other time is okay…)

'I'll be fine,' Noah answers with a shrug. 'I'd rather not order a cab and risk being recognized. At which point Mabel comes round long enough to agree about the importance of him remaining incontinent…

I cringe and hurriedly interject the word "incognito", but only half heartedly. For once I agree with my father. The prospect of such a famous personality drowning after having dinner at our house doesn't bear thinking about. 'Don't you worry about that lad, Jimmy will take you home and he'll keep his trap shut if he knows what's good for him.'

I can see that Noah is wondering who the hell Jimmy is, but all he says is, 'Gee, I don't want to put the poor guy out of his bed at this time of nigh…' But before he can get any further, the Admiral waves away his protests.

'Do him good, besides, he's already here – been sitting outside for the last hour – got to keep 'em in line don't you know.'

By this time I'm beginning to feel a bit light headed and

everything is taking on a dreamlike quality. I glance at Noah expecting to see derision in his gaze, but to my surprise, his return look is full of mirth and I can tell that, like before, he's actually enjoyed the whole exchange. Hesitantly I smile over at him as he rises from the sofa and he smiles back at me with barely restrained laughter. In my slightly inebriated state, the smile feels intimate and inviting and my heart thuds unevenly in response. As I follow the two men to the front door, I reflect that I will never forget this evening. In fact my mind has already begun fantasizing about our blossoming friendship; one that lasts through thick and thin; where he can't make a decision without me; flies me all over the world to keep him sane...

'Well Noah lad, it's been a pleasure and I've no doubt my daughter Victory feels the same. In fact I'd be very surprised if spending an evening with a fine specimen like you don't just tempt her back into the saddle...'

And just like that, the bubble bursts.

Saturday 3rd May

TO: kim@kimberleyharris.com

What time is it over there? It's late here but just had to tell you about the evening I just had. You wouldn't believe it - total riot.

Can you remember I told you about the house we're gonna be filming in? Well it was amazing, like something out of a Jane Austin novel, perfect for The Bridegroom.

The guy who owns the house (you know, the kooky Admiral - he told me his first name but apparently everyone calls him by his naval rank, even though he's been retired for years) was definitely one fry short of a Happy Meal and seemed to take great delight in doing everything he could to embarrass his daughter. Would you believe the poor girl's name is Victory! Apparently her father called her after some famous Admiral's ship – really need to dust off my British history. Mind you, the only person who calls her that is her dad, everyone else calls her Tory. She seemed pretty uptight the whole evening and spent most of it glaring at her father. She was (as mom used to say) a well built gal. Had a really nice smile though.

There was also another guest who (I guess) was the old guy's girlfriend. Seems a little weird calling her that, she must've been nearing seventy - think Miss Marple and you're getting the picture.

It was a bit strained at first, but once the Admiral got a few glasses inside him, he had some great stories, each one a bit more outrageous than the last. But the best bit was watching his daughter's response to each one. Priceless.

Just before I left, the Admiral announced he'd booked me a cab. I told him I didn't want anyone to know I was here and was happy to walk home (there's a track that follows the river), but the Admiral insisted that this guy called Jimmy would be delighted to take me and he wouldn't dare to breathe a word.

I was about to argue when the Admiral's girlfriend Mabel, who'd been asleep for the last hour, suddenly woke up and chipped in how important it was for me to stay incontinent. Hoping she meant incognito. Honest to God Kim, I don't know how I kept a straight face. Haven't had such an entertaining evening in ages. And to top it all, this guy Jimmy (who'd been waiting for me outside for over an hour – bizarre) got out of his car and actually saluted the old guy before opening the door for me to get in. Twenty minutes later we arrived at my house after total silence the whole way – Jimmy had apparently been instructed not to rabbit on – another one of those quaint British phrases meaning shut the fuck up....

As we pulled up at the house, I was just about to climb out when Jimmy suddenly thrust an old magazine cover under my nose with a full color shot of me semi naked and asked me to sign it for him so he could give it to his wife for their anniversary.

I tell you sis, you really couldn't make it up. British eccentricity at its very best.

Anyway, off to bed now. Feeling really mellow...

Noah xxx

Chapter Six

Sunday lunchtime in the Ship was always busy, much to Admiral Shackleford's disgust. In his opinion The Sunday Lunchers were in the same bracket as people who only went to church on Christmas Eve. Mind you, at least he wasn't a hypocrite he reflected as he wove his way through the crowd – he never went to church at all...

Arriving at the bar, the Admiral ordered his pint and glared at the upstart who had the temerity to sit on his stool. Eventually, as always, the look had the desired effect and the scoundrel got up and left. Laboriously seating himself down on the vacated seat with a grunt of satisfaction, the Admiral congratulated himself on still having a stare that could bring down a subordinate from thirty paces.

A few minutes passed by as he enjoyed his pint and reflected on the dinner party the night before. Then he glanced at his watch. Where the bloody hell was Jimmy? If the man was any later, he'd be considering disciplinary action – 'give 'em an inch and they take a mile' was the Admiral's firm philosophy.

Just then Jimmy pushed open the door with Pickles in tow. 'Sorry I'm late Sir,' he panted as he finally reached the bar. 'Emily wanted me to mow the lawn.' The Admiral frowned but decided against taking further action and waved at the barmaid to bring his friend a drink.

'So sir,' said Jimmy, climbing up on to his stool, 'how did last night go? Was it a success? Have to say the package seemed like he'd had a good time – not that we spoke a lot of course,' he hastened to assure the Admiral that he'd kept to the strict instructions.

Charles Shackleford grunted and took a draft of his pint before looking around to see if anyone was listening. There were advantages to a packed pub – even the barmaid didn't have the time to eavesdrop. Then he turned to Jimmy and grinned broadly. 'I think I can safely say that stage one of the plan is pretty much the dog's bollocks my friend. The package had a cracking time – although it has to be said that Victory was not her sparkling best.' He frowned slightly as he remembered his daughter's near continuous silence. 'Still, I threw out a couple of subtle hints to the package and am confident that by the end of the evening he could see past her miserable face and almost continuous drinking.

'Think we're on a roll Jimmy my lad, we're on a roll...'

Chapter Seven

'Oh my God, stop, please stop or I'm going to wet myself.' Kit is doubled over laughing as I give her the low down on last night. The unladylike snorting noises she's making are causing Dotty, who's curled up in her basket, to look up, head cocked to one side.

It's Sunday morning and we're both sitting in the little room at the back of Kit's art gallery. Housed on the ground floor of an old Tudor building on a pedestrianised street full of similar picture postcard buildings all converted into charming shops and cafes, the gallery is Kit's passion. It's actually owned by her absentee parents who show as much interest in the gallery as they do in their daughter – which is to say none. Most of the time, Kit's parents are a bit of a taboo subject and one we very rarely speak about. However, where the gallery is concerned, her parents' absence suits Kit fine as she gets to do with it as she wishes.

And I get to share the room at the back with her, which is where I run my Interior Design business. (I could do it equally well at home but… well, need I say more?)

The gallery is actually quiet for a Sunday in May, probably at least in part due to the recent run of sunny weather breaking in the early hours of this morning. The rain is now beating a frenzy against the windows in complete contrast to yesterday. It gives the old building a cosy feel, and the two of us time to chat, which ordinarily would be great, but on this occasion (Kit is now in fact crossing her legs in desperation she's laughing so hard) maybe not so much.

'I can't see what you find so funny,' I grouch. 'I told you he'd think we're all bonkers.' I daren't actually tell her about my father's clumsy attempts at matchmaking - just thinking about it is making me squirm with embarrassment, not to mention my school girl fantasies at the end of the evening...

Sighing, I cradle my mug of coffee and wait for my inconsiderate supposed best friend to get over her hysterics. After about five minutes she begins to sober up and sympathetically leans forward to give me a hug. Not ready to completely forgive her, I sniff and pull away on the pretexts of salvaging my coffee.

'Don't worry about it sweetheart, look at it this way, you've probably provided him with a story that will do the rounds of the rich and famous in Hollywood for the next ten years.'

'And that's supposed to make me feel better?' My voice has risen an octave. 'I can't believe you're being so insensitive about my humiliation.' Which of course starts her laughing again.

I'm just about to flounce out in my best Scarlett O'Hara impression when my mobile phone rings. Gritting my teeth I glance down at the number. It's one I'm not familiar with which means it could be business, so with one last glare at my former best friend, I turn my back to answer the call.

For a split second I don't recognize the male voice on the other end, then realization crashes in and my heart feels like it's going to burst out of my chest. Kit notices my stillness and immediately stops laughing to unashamedly eavesdrop.

'Hi Tory? It's Noah.' Oh my God, oh my God, oh my God.... 'It's *him*,' I mouth silently to her, pointing at the phone, our previous argument completely forgotten.

Kit frantically motions towards the speakerphone button as I simply stare at her dumbly, completely paralyzed. Frustrated, she makes a grab for the phone and we grapple briefly, eventually dropping the phone on the floor.

'Hello, hello? Is this Tory Shackleford's cell?' I can hear his voice faintly as we both make panicked eye contact before lunging to the floor at precisely the same time, resulting in our heads meeting with a resounding crack and both of us ending up on the floor with Dotty now barking excitedly between us.

Despite seeing stars, I manage to push Dotty away and grab the phone off the floor. Putting it back to my ear, I attempt a grunt followed by a wobbly, 'Just one moment please.' (Which I really hope will be enough of an indication that there is someone on this end of the line...)

I cover the mouthpiece with my other hand and groan. 'Bloody hell, that hurts,' echoes Kit, rubbing at the livid purple lump that has appeared on her forehead. I resist the urge to add my own expletive, take a couple of deep breaths and put the phone back to my ear.

'Hi Noah, sorry about that, I was just on the other line.' My voice doesn't sound too unsteady and feel quite proud of myself.

'Hope I'm not interrupting anything,' comes the cheerful response. 'Sounded like you were rolling around the floor with a dog – Dotty I presume.'

I attempt a tinkling, oh you are funny, kind of laugh which unfortunately comes out more of a cackle. For a split second I want to hang up and crawl under the table, then I glance over at Kit, still nursing her head, and she grins at me and makes a thumbs up sign.

'No, no, not at all.' Sounding quite normal now if I say so myself. 'It's lovely to hear from you. What can I do for you?'

'Well first of all I wanted to say thanks a bunch for having me round to dinner last night, it was great.' Kit's ear is now plastered next to mine and she rolls her eyes in disbelief. I retaliate by sticking my tongue out.

'You're very welcome,' I respond in my best Admiral Shackleford's daughter voice. Kit winces and I screw my eyes shut in an effort to block her out. There's a second's pause and I resist the urge to ask if we can do it again, just the two of us – tonight preferably...

Then he continues, and my heart literally jumps into my throat. 'Your dad mentioned last night that you fix up houses for a living?' His voice is a question but he continues without waiting for an answer. 'This house I'm renting. I love it. In fact I'm seriously thinking of buying. Problem is, it needs a hell of a lot of work and I was wondering if you'd like to come up and take a look.'

Well, bugger me. Noah Westbrook wants me to come and look at his house. For a moment I'm completely speechless

'What do I say?' I mouth at Kit who looks back at me like I've lost the plot, while miming 'duh' with her finger against her head.

'Err, what can I say? Err, I'd err love to. Err, when were you err thinking?' Obviously doesn't come out in my best "professional woman of the world" tone.

He doesn't appear to notice. 'That's great. How about Tuesday? The rest of the cast and crew are arriving at the end of the week and I won't have much time after that. Shall we say about four? Just in time for tea as you English say.' He laughs and parts of me that haven't seen daylight in years do a hop skip and a jump.

'I'm sure you understand if I ask you to keep this whole thing under wraps for now? Feel free to bring the pooch if you'd like.' I manage a faint 'Of course, thank you,' and he hangs up after promising to text me his address.

Kit and I remain sitting on the floor and stare at each other in silence. Then my phone makes a loud pinging noise, signaling receipt of a text message and we both burst out laughing uncontrollably.

~*~

Tuesday has finally arrived and I don't know whether to be hysterically happy or just hysterical. I spent most of Monday on the computer spying on the address Noah had given me using Google Maps. The aerial view showed me a large white gabled house directly overlooking the river Dart. From the road, all that could be seen was a large imposing front door with two stained glass windows either side. It looked like a bungalow, but the view from the road was merely the tip of the iceberg. The house was originally built to take full advantage of its position and the rest of it sprawled down towards the edge of the cliff with an uninterrupted view of the river and Dartmouth Castle on the other side. Manipulating the screen, my heart started to thud with excitement and enthusiasm that had nothing to do with Noah Westbrook. I totally got why he loved it so much and to be given free rein with such an amazing house would be a dream come true. I just knew I could do it justice.

That was yesterday. Between then and now, I have nearly talked myself out of going half a dozen times. However, a good half an hour talking to by Kit has convinced me that the possibility of looking a complete idiot is greater if I don't go than if I do...

After raining all day yesterday, we're now back to crisp and spring like – the sort of weather that makes you feel lucky to be alive. Obviously wanting to stay that way and knowing that the road winding around the cliffs at Kingswear has a tendency to be suicidally narrow in places - presenting unique challenges to anyone needing to park further than a few inches away from a hundred foot drop - I decide to walk. As a bonus, this will not only give me the opportunity to view the house from the outside with no interruptions but also do a runner before I'm seen if it all gets too much...

I settle on dressing sensibly (I haven't really got any other sort of clothes), determined to look professional. I go for straight jeans with sensible walking boots and a long crisp white shirt layered over the top which has the added advantage of making my hips and boobs look smaller. Finishing the whole ensemble off, I sling a sweater around my shoulders in my best old money impression. Kit would be proud of me.

Before heading towards the front door, I glance at myself critically in the mirror. My hair is going its own way as usual and I definitely look too pale despite my generous application of blusher and lipstick – nerves most likely kicking in. Still the walk will give me a healthy glow. I grab my portfolio and put it into my trusty satchel and make sure that Dotty is secured on the leash (don't want any odor issues today thank you very much)

Just as I'm about to leave, my father bangs out of his study yelling my name at the top of his voice. After debating long and hard, I decided against telling him about Noah's request - the potential for disaster far outweighing any possible advantage. In fact, over the years, I've learned not to trust my notoriously loose lipped father with anything remotely important. To be honest I'm at a loss to understand how there was never a serious military incident during my father's time as a Two Star, but possibly they hushed it up. Still, at the end of the day, he was only ever actually a Vice Admiral – we can all sleep safe in our beds secure in the knowledge that he was never promoted to Fleet Commander...

Turning round I slide my satchel behind my back - no idea why, it's not like he usually asks me where I'm going - however, on this occasion I must look guilty. 'You off somewhere?' His voice is suspicious and my heart sinks.

'Just heading down to the gallery, you know, busy busy...' I laugh falsely and back towards the door dragging Dotty with me. This is so not how it is normally. It's supposed to be the other way round. I'm an excellent inquisitor, but usually a terrible liar. But there we are, it's official – I really am a chip off the old block. All I need now is to have a bit more practice...

However, as I'm currently a complete novice at this lying lark, I turn and pull open the door, mutter a quick, 'Got to go,' and dash through, hauling Dotty's leash behind me. Unfortunately the door slams shut before she can get through it and I'm forced to re open it again. Popping my head back through I shout 'Bye,' quickly and yank Dotty's leash so hard, she practically shoots through the door in mid air.

Breathing a sigh of relief, I make my way down the gardens to the gate fronting the Dart and, passing the higher ferry slipway, begin the walk along the track at the side of the river.

The weather is perfect. There is a slight breeze causing billowy clouds to race across the sky creating alternately fantastical shadows and sparkling waves on the choppy water. The clank of ropes securing the moored up boats is the only sound as Dotty and I stride briskly along the pathway.

It takes us about fifteen minutes to reach Kingswear, we're making good time and I congratulate myself on my sensible decision to walk.

As we arrive at the village and begin the hike up the steep road winding around the headland, I smile to myself remembering the many times I did this as a child. Armed with a packed lunch, my friends and I would be gone for the whole day, following the footpath beyond the end of the road along the cliffs to the old gun casings, remnants from the Second World War. Overgrown and abandoned, they had provided a paradise for children with an imagination. I recall the many times I returned home dirty and disheveled just before dark to my mum's scolding. Dad always seemed to be away at sea.

As we continue the uphill climb I wonder how long it is since I've actually walked this far. I decide to take a break and lean against a wall a little out of breath. I don't remember the path being this steep when I was a child. I glance up at the sky. The clouds have disappeared entirely. It feels more like July. I shrug the Sloanie sweater off my shoulders and shove it into my satchel. Glancing down at Dotty, I can see she's panting slightly and I frown. Should have brought her some water.

I glance at my watch – three forty five already. Damn, I need to pick up the pace.

Ten minutes later I am not only the opposite of pale and interesting, I am hot, sweaty and my shirt is clinging to my back like I've just completed a marathon. The sun is beating down relentlessly and I'm beginning to feel light headed. Surely it can't be much further.

I decide to sit down and re establish my bearings. Parking myself on a large boulder under the welcome shade of a pine tree, I take a deep breath and, unbuttoning the bottom of my shirt, I flap the ends in an effort to bring some cool relief. Dotty luckily seems to be faring better than me and is sitting on a patch of grass unconcernedly nibbling her tail.

I am now five minutes late. Shielding my eyes, I squint up the road and see the outline of a dark figure walking towards us. I wonder if I can ask for directions without giving the game away, when suddenly Dotty jumps up and begins barking joyfully. I stop flapping, and shield my eyes again to try and see who it is.

As Dotty's barking reaches fever pitch, I suddenly realize exactly who it is. So much for viewing the property unobserved – and for actually failing to recognize said property. I stand up self consciously just as Noah Westbrook reaches us.

Which of course means I can't now do a runner, however strong the current urge... Dotty has no such desire and launches herself at the actor with complete abandon, all the while licking his face enthusiastically. I fumble with the buttons of my now limp shirt and wish I could do the same (of course the alternative would be to throw myself off the cliff...)

'I saw you stop through the window.' He gestures towards the house behind him with one hand while effortlessly holding the wriggling delighted dog with the other. 'Thought you seemed a little lost – not to mention tuckered out.'

Yep I think the throwing myself off the cliff option is definitely winning the battle. Ignoring my very obvious awkwardness, he holds out his spare hand and briefly touches my elbow. 'Come on, we'll have some tea before I show you around. I've put the kettle on.' He says the last bit with a boyish enthusiasm demonstrating his delight at being able to use the very English phrase in the correct context.

Then he turns and walks back to the house which I can now see is about ten yards away. My traitorous mongrel doesn't even glance behind her to see if I'm following. They are already at the gate before I'm able to get my feet to move from their current spot and as Noah glances back enquiringly over Dotty's head, I take a deep breath, grab my satchel and hurry after them.

I don't have any time to observe the front (or is it the back) of the house. Shutting the gate behind me, I scurry through the open door into the welcoming coolness of the lobby. Without putting Dotty down, he continues into a large square hall with a stunning spiral staircase to one side leading up to a galleried landing. The light in the hall is provided by a large glass atrium in the centre of the high ceiling casting a myriad of exquisite stained glass colours around the hall.

I know my mouth is open but I can't help myself. The hall is absolutely amazing. I can hear Noah chuckle at my reaction as he carries on through a door to the left of the staircase. Realising I've again been left alone, I hurry after him into a light airy room with floor to ceiling windows providing stunning views of the sloping lawn and of the river beyond.

'Oh my God,' I breathe, taking in the incredible panorama. I'm completely at a loss for words. I've always thought the Admiralty has lovely views, but they pale in comparison to this. I glance around the room and notice how bare it is, just a couple of sofas and a coffee table. I can feel my excitement begin to rise at the thought of being given a free rein in such an amazing house.

Eagerly, completely forgetting my earlier discomfort, I turn towards Noah, just as he is straightening up after gently putting a wriggling Dotty on to the floor. I'm about to wax lyrically about his wonderful house, but as he looks up towards me, I can see him clearly for the first time today and, for a few seconds, I am again struck dumb by his sheer masculine beauty. I note that he's barefoot, despite coming out in to the road, wearing only well worn jeans and a checked shirt, sleeves pushed up to reveal strong tanned forearms. With his hair tumbling in jet-black waves across his forehead, he looks like he's just climbed out of bed.

My gut clenches as I stare at him mesmerized. I feel just like the proverbial rabbit trapped in the headlights of an oncoming car... 'Would you like to freshen up a little before we take tea?' His words bring me back to earth with a bump and I glance down at myself in confusion.

My shirt is plastered to my breasts with sweat and the top has gaped open as a result of me playing with my buttons earlier. Face flaming, I groan slightly and frantically begin doing up buttons. Oh God, he probably thinks I'm coming on to him. I have absolutely no words that might possibly make this better. Without looking at him, I ask where the cloakroom is in a despondent whisper and simply follow his pointed arm.

Once in front of the mirror, I take a deep breath and look at my face and chest. Red, shiny, horribly sweaty and my best support bra for the fuller figure on full view. Miserably, I splash my face with cold water and finish doing up the rest of my buttons, all the while trying to pluck up the courage to go back out. Then all of a sudden I hear Dotty's insistent scratching and whimpering at the cloakroom door, and, looking at my reflection I find a smile from somewhere. At least my dog loves me.

'So what?' my evil inner voice responds, 'Did you actually think *he* might find you attractive?'

'Oh shut up,' I whisper venomously to my reflection, flipping my middle finger. Then I determinedly open the door and march back into the sitting room.

Chapter Eight

If Noah notices my shiny red face, he makes no sign, and waves me to the sofa opposite. He deftly pours the tea into china cups with all the skill of an honorary member of the Women's Institute. I busy myself taking a notebook and pen, as well as my portfolio, out of the satchel.

Dotty for once is showing her true colours by sitting snuggled up against me on the sofa (although I actually think it might be because the plate of biscuits is closer to my side of the coffee table...)

As we sit and chat about ideas for the house, I slowly relax, and I can feel myself become more animated. Interior Design is my world and I know I'm good at it. I lay examples of previous projects onto the coffee table which beautifully illustrate my skill (Dartmouth is certainly not short of big houses with big money.) Noah doesn't say much as he studies the photographs and allows me to wax lyrically about them.

When I finally run out of words, I wonder if I've overdone it. After all, this guy is used to Hollywood luxury. What can a provincial interior designer from the wilds of south Devon possibly show him that's new and different? I sort of expect him to politely show me to the door, after promising to 'give me a call sometime'. To my surprise, he does no such thing. Standing up, he offers to show me around the rest of the house and I resist the urge to clap my hands in excitement (My behaviour's not normally this erratic but then it's not every day one gets to sit and discuss wallpaper with the world's sexiest man).

I get up, clutching my notebook in a death grip and finally notice that Dotty's wandered off somewhere. I don't worry too much, figuring we'll find her on our tour. 'Ready when you are. I'll make notes as we go.'

The rest of the house is mostly empty and as Noah leads me through each room, I can feel my uncertainty slip away and my excitement rise. Light and airy, the architect obviously built the house to make the most of the light, and nearly all of the rooms have uninterrupted views of the sloping lawn and the River Dart beyond. Feverishly scribbling ideas into my notebook, I'm in my element, totally swept away by the rising tide of anticipation and eagerness that always accompanies a new project, especially one as unique as this.

Finally we're at the door to the master bedroom. His bedroom. The door is slightly ajar, and just as I'm about to push it open, ridiculously I falter, my reluctance quite obvious. My heart begins to thumping so loudly, I'm sure he can hear it. As I stand with my back to him, willing myself to stop being such a prude, a mobile phone rings downstairs and I breathe a sigh of relief as he heads off to answer it, telling me to go on without him.

I open the door the rest of the way with a determined shove and come face to face with an unmade super king sized bed completely dominating the bedroom. Against my will, I imagine the two of us naked and tangled amid the rumpled Egyptian cotton sheets and I swallow convulsively, trying to rid myself of the all too vivid image before he returns.

Then suddenly the sheet moves and I automatically recoil, taking an involuntary step backwards, all carnal thoughts taking immediate flight. Slowly the sheet undulates. 'What the…,' I mutter, taking another step back, just as Dotty's head pops out next to the pillow.

'Bloody hell Dotspot, what on earth are you doing?' My whisper is heated as I walk towards the bed intending to grab my unruly animal and escape.

Unfortunately Dotty has other ideas and darts to the other side of the bed where she eyes me with mischief, bottom in the air and tail wagging enthusiastically. I groan, knowing that catching her in such a large expanse is not going to be easy – especially when she's in this mood. I slowly creep around the other side, all the while looking the other way in the hope of catching her unawares.

She's done this before, and each time my grab meets with thin air. Any minute now she's going to start barking and I'll find out first hand just what Noah Westbrook thinks of having dogs in his bed. I hold my hand up to her in an attempt to prevent the inevitable and then take one last lunge across the bed. I actually nearly manage to grasp the end of her tail before I crash full length across the mattress, just as Dotty disappears under the frame.

My first thought is 'shit' followed closely by 'I'll kill her.' Scooting forward on my stomach, I grasp the edge of the bed to look underneath.

'Looking for dust?' My head snaps up so quickly I could possibly sue him for whiplash, and I stare in horror at the legs and feet in front of me. Damn, damn, damn, I didn't hear him come back upstairs.

Swallowing again, I have a brief second to note that his feet are actually as attractive as the rest of him before my gaze continues upward in apprehension. I simply stare at him mutely. What possible excuse can I give for being on his bed?

Then my disobedient dog's head pops out from underneath the mattress along with a joyful bark and he quickly weighs up the situation. Before he can speak, I make an effort to scramble into a sitting position and scoop Dotty up at the same time, all the while mumbling my abject apologies. Bugger, I'm still wearing my trainers. I attempt to swing my legs around without getting my dirty shoes on his pristine white sheets and in doing so, horror of horrors, I can feel myself begin to slide off the bed. I'm still holding on to Dotty, and am now in grave danger of landing on my head.

Noah (who has remained ominously silent thus far) quickly crouches down and grabs hold of my shoulders so my head is now cradled in his crutch and I'm staring up into his impassive face. How the hell did I get to be in this position...?

We stare at each other for a few seconds and I note whimsically that his eyes are actually the colour of sapphires, then Dotty breaks the spell by wriggling loose, and jumping up to give him a resounding lick on the nose.

I struggle to right myself with my legs still on the mattress and Noah tries to help by pushing my shoulders off his nether regions. Unfortunately, as I'm not exactly sylph like, this takes more effort than perhaps he's bargained for. By the time I've managed to swing my legs off the bed and he's shoved me into a sitting position, we're both panting like we've just finished a twenty minute workout. It's the most exercise I've had in ages...

I turn round on my knees to face him. 'I'm so,so sorry Noah. I didn't know Dotty was on your bed, I was just trying to get her off then I fell and she went under the bed and then I saw you and managed to grab her and then I started to fall and...' I know I'm babbling and probably sound like a complete lunatic (oh God am I taking after my father?)

Unbelievably the actor smiles ruefully and, standing up, he waves my apologies away. 'Don't worry about it. I've been in much more compromising positions than this. Tell me what you'd like to do with this bedroom.'

Telling myself sternly that he means *to it*, not *in it,* I resist the urge to ask him what kinds of compromising positions and get to my feet, determined to make no more embarrassing faux pas. Smoothing my shirt down, I rescue my notebook from the bedside table, glance down at my scribbles and cough self consciously – all the while chanting 'professional, professional' inside my head... Then, taking a deep breath I tell him.

Half an hour later we are again ensconced in the drawing room, as I've referred to it in my notes, and my embarrassment has been completely replaced by enthusiasm. Hoping against hope that I haven't completely blown it, I give him all my initial thoughts and ideas – including a completely new state of the art kitchen, the possible building of an Edwardian style conservatory on the side of the house and a New England type porch spanning the whole of the front. Might as well go for broke seeing as money is not actually an issue…

Twenty minutes in to my animated dialogue, I can see he's hooked. He leans forward and his eyes really do begin to sparkle and suddenly he seems so much more approachable. For the first time I forget he's a famous Hollywood movie star and just see him as a prospective client with a beautiful house that I *know* I can turn into something amazing.

When I finally trail off into silence, he stares out at the wonderful views and nods his head without speaking. It's obvious that some internal battle is being played out in his head and I long to ask him why he's even considering buying a house here of all places. Beautiful it undoubtedly is, but I sense that on some level he's actually running away from something and my curiosity is inevitably roused. What's he doing here all alone? Is that normal for someone like him? Despite the questions whirling around in my head, for once in my life I remain silent.

I sense that any attempt to pry into his private life will be met with open hostility and I wonder what it must be like to be constantly in the public eye – every decision, every movement scrutinized and analyzed remorselessly. Unobserved, I sit and watch his beautiful but remote face and wonder if there is someone in his life. He looks so sad and lonely. Ridiculously I find myself wanting to give him a hug, just to show him that everything will be okay. How crazy is that?

Just as I'm beginning to wonder if he's forgotten I'm here, Dotty - never one to be ignored for long - decides to put an end to the silence by jumping sneakily on to the coffee table and helping herself to a biscuit. I scold her half heartedly, for once secretly glad she's such a hog. The quiet was definitely becoming oppressive.

Visibly rousing himself from his reverie, Noah simply smiles down at the little dog and hands her another one. Then looking over at me sitting nervously on the edge of the sofa he smiles again, this time warmly and directs the full force of his charm at little old me. Just like that he turns back into Noah Westbrook, Hollywood heart throb.

'I love your ideas. Can you sketch them out for me?' I nod my head vigorously, not trusting myself to speak. 'Do you want more tea or would you prefer something a little stronger?'

Inexplicably my heart begins thudding in my chest and I nod my head again. 'Is that a yes for tea or a yes for a glass of wine?' His tone is now teasing and intimate. (Am I imagining this?)

'Wine, please,' I manage to croak, wondering if I'll ever have the opportunity to become blasé in his company.

He heads into the kitchen, and brings back a bottle and two glasses. 'Pinot Noir okay?' At my nod, he deftly uncorks the wine, and pours two large measures. Taking my glass from his hand, I reflect that it's a good job I'm not driving, and take a large gulp. As expected, the wine is full bodied and smooth so I take another very large, very appreciative mouthful and all but smack my lips (not that we drink bad wine in our house you understand, but after forty years in the Royal Navy my father is quite happy to drink anything that is remotely alcoholic...) And this little number has probably cost the equivalent of a two week all inclusive in The Maldives...

I'm beginning to feel very mellow and relaxed. Peering into my glass, I'm surprised to see that it's actually nearly empty and, ever the perfect host, Noah leans forward to fill it up. There is quiet as he looks over my portfolio again. I'm really not good with silence and I frantically think of something to say.

'I'm really sorry about your bed.' Apologizing again – really grasping at straws. 'It was incredibly rude of me to lay on it without asking.'

He looks up with a quirky smile before answering drily, 'You'd be surprised how many women I find in my bed uninvited.' I feel my face flame and stutter, 'Well, of course I wasn't, I mean I didn't, I mean it wasn't...'

Unexpectedly he laughs. 'I know, don't worry about it Tory, it's not a big deal.'

My face reddens again at his use of my name. 'For God's sake get a grip girl,' I admonish myself taking another gulp. 'How long will you be working on The Bridegroom?' I ask finally, congratulating myself on coming up with a safe topic.

'It depends on lots of factors, but we should be wrapped up by the end of the year.'

'Oh. So when will you finish filming here in Dartmouth? It will be so strange to see our house on the big screen. When is the film going to be released?' I'm babbling again...

This time he closes my portfolio decisively before looking up again– way to go Victory, piss him off with endless questions. 'We'll be filming in Dartmouth until the end of this month and the movie is scheduled for release next summer. You'll probably hardly recognize your house in the movie when you see it, they'll no doubt make lots of changes. Remember, it's supposed to be the nineteenth century.'

He doesn't actually sound pissed. 'Will you be living here permanently?' I can't help it, it just slips out. I bite my lip and take another gulp of wine thinking stupid, stupid, stupid.

To my surprise he answers me. 'I'm not totally sure. I have lots of things going on in my life right now.' He smiles ruefully. 'Think maybe I'm looking for somewhere to hole up if I'm honest, as far away from tinsel town as I can get.'

I am so gob smacked that he's actually answered my question that I really can't think of anything to say back. I just stare at him, again seeing the slight sadness behind his eyes.

Then the moment is lost as he raises his glass and speaks with a determined grin, all the melancholy gone. 'So come on Victory Shackleford, where does a guy go to have fun around here?'

My mind briefly pictures me showing him the bright lights of Dartmouth – it certainly won't take long – then I remember, 'Well, there is a music festival at the end of May,' I say excitedly, 'if you're still here then. It lasts for three days and is usually great fun. There's live music in every pub and on the bandstand in the park. I doubt anyone will recognize you if you go, it's usually heaving.'

'Sounds like a blast,' Noah responds with what seems like

genuine enthusiasm. 'If we get a break from filming, I'll tag along if you don't mind.'

'Th..that would be lovely.' I'm stuttering again, all the while chanting 'It's not a date, it's not a date' inside my head... Dotty chooses that moment to let out a little whine and I know she wants to go to the bathroom. She's abandoned the biscuits and is sitting next to the double doors leading out on to the terrace.

'Would you like to see the rest of the garden before you leave?' I jump at his offer, sensing our intimacy is at an end and if I hang around much longer, I'll be outstaying my welcome. 'Great,' I smile, standing up hurriedly, 'Lead on.'

Twenty minutes later Dotty and I are back on the road. I am on cloud nine. If there was a ten, I'd be on it. I've left my portfolio with Noah with the proviso I'll collect it when I bring him my ideas for the house.

Which I'm going to leave with him at *the cocktail party he's holding for the cast and crew this Saturday.* I'm actually skipping down the road – Dotty is running after me in bewilderment. I can't believe I've been invited. Victory Shackleford hobnobbing with the rich and famous. My steps falter slightly as I remember that Noah has also invited my father and I wonder what bribe I can use to get him to behave.

Maybe agree to move out? Yep, that should do it...

~*~

I spend the last half an hour of my walk back wondering how on earth I'm going to broach the subject of Noah's invitation without admitting I've been up to his house, finally settling on the admittedly weak story of bumping into Noah in town. Sadly I'm incapable of coming up with anything more elaborate – I really have got a long way to go to get to my father's level of proficiency at telling a good cock-and-bull story.

Unfortunately I think he might have been lying in wait for me at the house because he throws open the door just as I'm about to put my key in. Pickles immediately barrels out, launching himself delightedly at Dotty as if they've been apart for days – elderly he may be, but he certainly hasn't lost his eye for the ladies. Mind you, I can't help but reflect that the term lady in this instance might be stretching it a bit as I watch Dotty enthusiastically throwing herself onto her back...

In an effort to postpone the inevitable, I bend down to rub Pickles' ears and pick Dotty up. As I finally straighten back up, my father clears his throat self consciously, and I look up as my internal alarm bells immediately begin to ring. My father is many things but self conscious is not one of them. I know this from first hand, very painful experience... 'Err, I was wondering, thought we might have a bit of a chat – you know, father and daughter like.'

I thought back to the last time we had a bit of a father daughter chat which lead to him writing me off as an uptight poker arsed spinster. Still, it will give me a chance to put forward Noah's invitation. Maybe he won't be able to go to the party. Could be he just wants to tell me he's intending a dirty (sorry, romantic) weekend with Mabel. My hopes somewhat lifted, I nod my head and we retire to Dad's study, which has been the traditional place for our one-to-ones since I was first out of nappies.

I sit myself down with Dotty on my knee as my father begins to pace, mumbling to himself. I frown slightly. This is getting weirder and weirder. Then the thought suddenly hits me. Oh God, please tell me he's not thinking of marrying Mabel Pomfrey – not yet. Unbidden, I see a vision of me walking down the aisle as maid of honour behind my soon to be stepmother.

'So Victory, what d'you think of him then? Come on girl, and don't give me any flannel.'

My vision is now in full Technicolor – I'm wearing lilac. Then I frown as his words sink in. 'Think of who?'

'Now don't act dense with me Victory Shackleford. You know who I'm talking about. The actor chap, you know, the looker. Tell it me straight. What do you think of him? Is he the kind of bloke you could see yourself bunking up with?'

I stare at my father's earnest *and very serious* face. I have no idea what to say.

'I mean, you'd probably have to move across the Pond but he's not short of a bob or two so he'd let you come home from time to time and 'course me and Mabel can come over and visit...'

He trails off, probably in response to the look of abject horror on my face. 'Have you been drinking?' Is all I can think of to say.

He sighs dramatically at my apparent refusal to answer his question and plonks himself into the chair opposite.

'Fair do, could be I'm jumping the gun a tad but it has to be said you're a bit like a fart in a trance at the best of times my girl and as I'm your father, I want what's best for you. So, DO YOU WANT TO MARRY THIS BLOKE OR NOT?'

There is silence for a few seconds as my head attempts to make sense of his last sentence. Then I explode.

'Are you completely off your rocker? Of course I don't want to marry him you idiotic old wind bag. I've only known him for five minutes. Do I fancy the pants off him? Damn right I do, but then so does every other female with a working pulse. If you do anything at all to embarrass me at this party, so help me I really will throttle you.'

'Party, what party?'

I open my mouth to start up again and realize that I really have done it. There is absolutely no chance my stupid stupid STUPID father is going to cry off from the invitation now. Oh no, not when he's on a mission to marry his fat, plain spinster of a daughter off to a famous movie star. God, he must want rid of me badly if he's prepared to cook up such a crazy scheme. I have never been so angry and hurt.

I stand up, place a now shivering Dotty on to the floor and walk over to where he's sitting. Putting a hand on each arm of the chair, I lean forward and speak softly, slowly and clearly.

'You and I have been invited to a social event at Noah Westbrook's house on Saturday evening along with most of the film crew and actors filming here in The Bridegroom. The purpose I believe is to kick off their time in Dartmouth with a light hearted little bash before the hard work of the next few weeks begins on Monday.

You will behave and you will refrain from saying or doing *anything* even remotely hinting at the possibility of a future relationship between Noah and me. If you go against my wishes in this, I promise you dad, hand on heart, that you will NEVER get me to move out of this house. The party begins at seven thirty.'

Then straightening up, I walk carefully out of the room without looking back.

My father never says a word.

Tuesday 6th May

TO: kim@kimberleyharris.com

Hey Kimmy, sorry haven't been in touch for a couple days, been catching up on my lines before we kick off next week. How's it going in sunny LA? Kids and Ben OK?

I've sort of come to a decision – drum roll... Think I'm gonna go ahead and buy the house I'm renting.

Before you go all crazy on me sis, hear me out. I won't move here permanently, but it's somewhere I can hole up when it all gets too much and the thing is, I just love it here. It's like being on a totally different planet and after what happened, I really need that.

Please don't think I'm abandoning you and the kids, I just need time to figure things out in my head. I know you understand.

You remember Tory Shackleford? Well turns out she decorates stuff – pretty good at it too. She came over earlier and had some great ideas for making over the house. It was great to have a conversation with somebody who's not trying to second guess me all the time, you know, someone who's not afraid to give an opinion, be damned whether I like it or not. Seems like she got quite a lot of spunk when she's not so uptight.

Anyhow my peace will be shattered at the end of this week with the crew and cast descending. I've decided to throw a party on Saturday evening to get all the guys together. Not sure why now to be honest – guess it seemed like a good idea at the time. Think I was hoping Gaynor would still be in Barbados, but no such luck. David said she was – and I quote – 'the fucking leading lady' and to get her ass over to the UK. Apparently that means they need her back as soon as possible. She's no doubt sulking her way over the Atlantic as we speak...

Anyway gotta go – catering to sort out. Don't worry about me will you? I won't do anything stupid sis and promise I won't drop off the face of the earth ;-)

Missing you loads

Noah xxx

Chapter Nine

'Well, I've made a tactical error Jimmy and no mistake. In fact you would be closer to the mark if you called it a complete balls up. You'd think a fellow like me who's given so much to international diplomacy over the years would not have cocked up quite so royally...' The Admiral glanced irritably over at Jimmy who all of a sudden began spluttering and coughing into his pint. 'What the bloody hell's wrong with you?' he asked crossly before sighing impatiently and hammering the smaller man on the back. 'I'm buggered if I'm going to give you the kiss o' life Jimmy, so you better pull yourself together.'

Taking a few deep breaths, Jimmy managed to stem the coughing fit – possibly due to the horrible thought of potentially being resuscitated by a balding, pot bellied sixty five year old man.

The two men had eschewed their usual seats at the bar in favour of a secluded corner of the Ship where they were less likely to be overheard – even though at four in the afternoon the pub was almost empty, not to mention the sounds of Pickle's snoring at their feet could potentially drown out a fog horn.

'Don't be too hard on yourself Sir,' Jimmy managed finally, 'We all know that Tory can be a prickly character. You gave it your best shot, there's no shame in giving up.'

'What the bloody hell are you talking about man? Give up? 'Course I'm not giving up. Just showed me cards too damn soon.' The Admiral sighed again, this time petulantly. 'Admittedly it is a bit of a crippler, but she's definitely got the hots for the package, I can tell you that much.'

There was a pause as both men went back to their pints.

'And we've got this bash tomorrow. That's it…' The Admiral banged his now empty pint decisively on the table causing Pickles to wake up with a start. Turning to Jimmy, he pointed his finger at the smaller man in excitement. Gone was the petulant voice to be replaced by a passionate zeal.

'What bash?' interjected Jimmy bewildered, only to be ignored as the Admiral went into overdrive.

'I think it's time subtlety went out the window Jimmy. It's time to bring out the big guns. I'm going to turn on the old charm.' He ignored Jimmy's look of horror and stood up. 'Got to go Jimmy my man. Pick us up at seven.' And with that he strode out, a man with renewed purpose.

Jimmy looked down at Pickles still sitting on the floor at his feet. 'What bash?' He asked the dog weakly, 'And what am I going to tell Emily? I'm supposed to be taking her to bingo.'

Chapter Ten

Since my heady brush with Hollywood I've spent most of every day holed up in Kit's back office feverishly bringing my ideas for Noah Westbrook's house to life. I've hardly been home except to eat and sleep, especially since the house is now filled with techies getting ready to begin filming next week, not to mention the posse of fans that now seem to be permanently camped outside our garden gate.

However, truth is, the main reason I've been staying away is to avoid my idiot father who I am delighted to say I haven't seen since our conversation on my return from Noah's on Tuesday. Unfortunately not seeing him has not stopped me from thinking about him, or rather fretting about what he's up to. Burying myself in my work has helped, but ever since our little "chat", my delight at being invited to Noah's cocktail party has been tempered by a deep foreboding that is getting worse by the day. And now it's Friday; the party is tomorrow and the foreboding has turned to downright dread. I'm even considering slipping a couple of sleeping pills into my father's pre-party drink. Or I could lock him in the cellar. That's how desperate I am.

Despite Kit's frantic pleas, I have thus far resisted her efforts to get me another new outfit. She doesn't know about the chat and I can't bring myself to tell her. I think maybe it has to do with the secret fantasies I couldn't help harbouring the last time I saw Noah. Admitting them would make me as ridiculous as my father and buying something new would signify hope.

The dress I bought for the dinner will do fine.

Against my will, I find myself going over the conversation with dad for the hundredth time, which of course only adds to my apprehension. Luckily, before I become too depressed, my reverie is interrupted by Kit who's been tied up in the gallery all day. She looks tired. 'Phew, I'm totally wiped,' she groans, confirming my prognosis as she flops down in to the other chair. 'Thank God the day's nearly over. I could murder a drink.'

I glance at my watch, surprised to notice that it's after five pm already. 'Have you closed up yet?' I ask, gathering my notes together.

'Yep, all done and dusted. You fancy a quick one in the Cherub?' As I hesitate, glancing back down at my work, she goes on to say in a more wheedling tone 'Think Freddy is going to be there...'

Freddy is the other third of our triangle and I've known him for as long as Kit. His real name is actually Gerald – but, as he so succinctly put it – who ever heard of a gay Gerald? He took his idol's name when he came out at sixteen and both Kit and I were there to shield him from the worst of the taunts. He now works "in theatre darling". Unfortunately, the theatre is the local Arts Centre in Dartmouth. He's ever hopeful that he'll be whisked away to the bright lights of London - although when we ask him why he doesn't just up sticks and go, he responds with, 'What will you do without me sweetie?'

I think the reality is he's more than happy to be a big fish in a very small pond. He's been away in Spain for the last three weeks ostensibly interviewing a Spanish Ballet troupe for a possible interpretation of Carmen in the autumn.

'When did he get back from Seville?' I ask, torn between wanting to see Freddy and holing up in a dark corner somewhere

'About thirty minutes ago. I had a text.' She opens her phone to read me Freddy's message.

'Spent debauched week with hot Spaniard. Think I'm in love. Meet me in Cherub at six. P.S. Tell Tory. Kiss, kiss, kiss.' Obviously he didn't just assess the dancing... Still, her impression of Freddy's nasally tones has me smiling for the first time today.

I glance down at Dotty who has been so good all day, still lying quietly in her basket even though her legs must now be in plaits. I know I've neglected her over the last few days, and she absolutely adores Freddy.

'Okay, you're on.' I grin finally, giving in. 'I'll just give Dotty some dinner and pop to the bathroom to freshen up.'

Ten minutes later we're out of the door and on our way to the oldest pub in Dartmouth. Unfortunately it actually takes us twenty minutes to do what is usually a five minute walk at the most – and that's despite taking a short cut past the church and The Seven Stars pub. Everyone in Dartmouth is consumed by the prospect of a big Hollywood blockbuster being filmed in the town (although "town" is stretching it a bit given that our house is actually over the other side of the river). I think every Dartmothian and his dog fancies himself as a budding thespian and by the time we reach the Cherub, I have been handed fifteen telephone numbers 'just in case they need any extras.' I actually think Freddy could make some money as an agent...

The final straw comes just before we reach our destination. Kit is just about to push open the door when old Mr Higgins decides to favour us with his own unique interpretation of Hamlet. Luckily I manage to restrain Kit from lamping an old age pensioner and he gets as far as 'Alas poor Yor!' before I shut the door in his face.

Breathing a sigh of relief, I pick Dotty up as Kit and I wait for our eyes to adjust to the welcoming dimness of the pub's interior.

'Once more unto the breach, dear frien...Ow.' Kit throws her handbag at Freddy who is sitting grinning in the corner. Recognizing his voice, Dotty instantly begins barking excitedly and struggles to get out of my arms. Laughing, I let her go and she dashes over to Freddy in a whirlwind of wagging tail and ecstatic little yaps.

'Hello pooch,' says Freddy, equally delighted to see Dotty and, holding the wriggling dog up in front of him, he allows her to lick his nose.

As Kit and I follow her to the table, I notice there's already an open bottle of Champagne with three empty glasses. 'What's the occasion?' Kit asks, plonking herself on a stool, thus subtly leaving the chair for my more ample bottom...

Freddy carefully tucks Dotty in next to him before he turns his attention back to us. 'Well, given that our dear Tory is now hobnobbing with the rich and famous over at the Admiralty, I thought I'd help her get used to their tipple of choice.'

'You know naaathing,' retorts Kit in her best Manuel from Fawlty Towers impression, while wasting no time pouring the bubbly into our glasses.

'Mmm, intriguing,' murmurs Freddy leaning forward conspiratorially. 'Do tell...'

'Well, where do I start?' Kit wiggles her eyebrows and holds up her glass. 'To our darling Victory who is well overdue for a fairytale...'

'Oh my God, you've shagged someone. Finally.' Freddy turns to me elatedly. 'I want to hear everything, spare no gory detail...'

'I haven't shagged anybody,' I snap, glaring at Kit who simply raises her eyebrows again and continues to drink her Champagne. Sighing, I take a sip of my drink. This is likely to take a while.

By the time I finish, Freddy is sitting enthralled with his chin balanced on his hands. 'It *is* a fairytale,' he breathes, clapping his hands together. 'I love it. The sexiest man in the whole world is going to sweep in and claim our Victory. I can feel it, deep down in my jingly bits.' I open my mouth to interrupt but he forestalls me by raising his glass again. 'Dear, dear girl, if it can't be me jumping Noah Westbrook's bones, then there's no one else who deserves it more...' Kit holds up her glass in agreement and I finally crack.

'You're both acting like complete morons.' I say through gritted teeth. 'You're as bad as my father.' Then I grab the

Champagne bottle, slosh its contents into my glass and knock it back in one before putting my head despairingly into my hands.

I can sense Kit frowning. 'What's wrong Tory? You've not been yourself all week. You know we're only teasing – we're both dead jealous really.' I look back up as she puts her hand on my shoulder. 'There *is* something wrong Victory Shackleford, I know you too well. Come on girl, spill the beans.'

Freddy puts his hand on my other shoulder and even Dotty whines slightly. Looking round at them all, suddenly the funny side of the whole thing hits me. I feel like I'm in an episode of Eastenders. Any minute now the closing theme is going to start...

I start to laugh and all three of them recoil slightly, a bit shocked at my sudden change of mood – I think they're beginning to worry I might be slightly deranged. The thought just makes me laugh harder.

'What's so funny?' Kit finally asks in an offended tone. 'We're only trying to help.'

'Oh my God, you've no idea,' I gasp before launching into more hysterical laughter.

'I think she's having a seizure,' Freddy mutters, eyeing me with concern. He comforts Dotty who is now shivering and staring at me anxiously. With a gargantuan effort, I reduce my guffaws to titters and wipe my now streaming eyes. 'I'm so sorry,' I whisper, 'There's something I haven't told you. I just couldn't bring myself to, but the thing is, I'm so scared he's going to do something awful.'

Half an hour later Freddy orders another bottle of Champagne. And chips.

In the end it's gone eight o'clock before Dotty and I are on the Higher Ferry. Cuddling the little dog to me I decide that it really is true that a problem shared is a problem halved. What the hell does it matter if my father makes a complete tit of himself? It's only a bloody party for goodness sake. And anyway, the chances of someone like Noah Westbrook being interested in someone like me are absolutely zero. Even if he goes ahead and buys the house, odds are he'll hardly ever live in it and when he does, I certainly won't know about it. I am totally getting myself worked up for nothing. I've just got to get the next few weeks over with and then my life can go back to normal.

As we arrive at the other side, I get the first surprise of the evening. Our tatty, sagging gate at the bottom of the garden has been replaced with a swanking six foot metal contraption that will no doubt keep out even the most determined paparazzi. I frown and give it a shake before noticing a small box to the left. An intercom, how exciting. Leaning forward, I press the button and after a few seconds, a male voice I don't recognize asks me for my name. 'Victory Britannia Shackleford,' I answer, thinking I'd better take it all very seriously in case they decide to shoot me. There's a short pause as I hear someone in the background muttering, 'What kind of a fuck name is that?' Closely followed by, 'Shit, it's the daughter.'

I can only agree with both sentiments, and ten minutes later Dotty and I are doing our usual huffing and puffing routine up the garden path, (well I am anyway). However, as I get nearer to the house, I stop in astonishment and stare at the second surprise of the evening. Our slightly scruffy garden terrace and the grass around it have been transformed into a perfect example of exquisitely groomed nineteenth century splendour. It looks beautiful, exuding an almost otherworldly eeriness in the deepening twilight. It would be easy to believe we've actually stepped back in time.

'Wow,' I breathe down to Dotty who doesn't appear to share my awe and is busy relieving herself over the expertly manicured flower bed. I drag her away, scanning the windows of the house to see if any of the film crew are still around.

'You've got no class,' I mutter to the little dog as we make our way around to the back door. Inside the house has not been changed quite as much but everything is now gleaming and the smell of polish and paint is so strong it makes me sneeze. 'Someone's had a busy day,' I reflect as I make my way upstairs to my bedroom. Mind you I was expecting the hall to be littered with expensive camera equipment but either they've stored their equipment elsewhere in the house or they don't trust us to look after it…

I breathe a sigh of relief as I enter my bedroom. This room really is my sanctuary and I've made it quite clear (to everybody and his dog) that under no circumstances is it to be used during filming. Not that they would want to really. The slightly shabby interior has hardly changed since I was a girl and everywhere my mother's touch is evident. When I'm in this room, I can almost believe she's still here.

~*~

It's Saturday morning. I've had the first good night's sleep since dad dropped his bombshell about The Bridegroom. I can hear muted noises from downstairs indicating that at least some of the crew are working over the weekend and glancing down at my watch I'm surprised to see it's still only eight thirty.

The sun is streaming in through the gap in the curtains and I'm tempted to jump out of bed and throw them wide. I really am a morning person. Dotty on the other hand most definitely is not, and usually has to be dragged out of bed. Right now she's still snoring loudly, dead to the world. Smiling, I put off letting the morning sunlight in and turn over to spoon with her little warm furry body. She sighs contentedly without opening her eyes and, as I kiss the top of her head, I can't help but wonder if I'll ever get to do this with a body that's only got hair on the interesting bits...

By ten o'clock, even Dotty's cast iron bladder is about to give up the ghost and after extracting herself from her warm cocoon, she is waiting by the door as I come out of the shower. Dressing quickly, I head downstairs to let her out the front door. Despite the noise I heard earlier, there's no one in the hall. I can hear Pickles barking from the depths of the study but I really am in no hurry to see my father despite my mini epiphany last night, so

I decide instead to follow Dotty into the garden to have another look in full daylight (and to make sure Dotty doesn't dig up the immaculate flower beds).

As I wander around the terrace, I'm suddenly consumed with excitement at the thought of seeing our house on the silver screen. This is the first time I've looked at the whole thing as other than a major encumbrance (apart from the obvious – tea with a famous screen idol etc...) It really is actually quite thrilling and I determine there and then that I'm going to stop moaning and just relax and enjoy the whole experience.

Calling Dotty, I walk round towards the back door into the kitchen humming to myself, and, pushing open the door, come face to face with Mabel entertaining two strange men in *my* kitchen. I stop so suddenly that Dotty bumps into my legs, then she skips around me and begins barking furiously at the visitors. I can hear Pickles' answering barks accompanied by frenzied whining and scratching at the study door, which suddenly opens. Any minute now my father is going to come stomping in demanding what that bloody racket is. Oh joy, now we can have a proper party.

My hard won serenity is disappearing faster than you can say Dalai Lama and, as my father throws open the kitchen door and strides in with Pickles hard at his heels, I'm right back to square one...

'This is my daughter Victory,' he booms to the two visitors.

'Tory,' I interject faintly, more out of habit than because anyone is listening.

'I can see you've met Mabel.' Unbelievably he smacks her ample bottom. 'Have you put the kettle on my dove? Then, turning back to our guests, 'Now don't you mind our Victory's miserable face. It's perfectly normal for her to look like she's been chewing on a wasp.'

The two men are looking increasingly bewildered. Mabel is tittering and Dotty is now trying to hump Pickles' leg in excitement. Situation normal really...

Striding round the table, I decide to take charge. So I plaster a smile on my face (the wasp jibe definitely stung a bit!) and hold out my hand towards the two men. 'Tory Shackleford, so pleased to meet you. I assume you're both part of the crew?' I'm now grinning broadly and, as one of the men shrinks back slightly, I realize I might be slightly overdoing it.

Still, they both stand up and shake hands informing me their names are Jed and Arnold (Arnold?) Both are most definitely Brits and when I express surprise, they tell me it's quite normal for more minor members of a film crew to be taken on where the shoot takes place. Breathing a sigh of relief that they're only "minor", I ask them what their jobs are while pouring water into the kettle. Unfortunately they go all techie on me and I have to admit to zoning out as I busy myself making tea. However I do manage to get they really are new to this crew and haven't actually met any of the big guns yet – better and better...

Relaxing slightly, I take the teapot and milk to the table along with some croissants and jam. 'Can you grab some cups Mabel?' I ask the older woman who unbelievably is still giggling like she's on a first date. Giggling should definitely be banned after the age of twenty. I know my voice is a bit snarky and I also know that she won't know where the cups are – I'll show the geriatric father stealer whose kitchen this is...

Unfortunately she appears to know exactly where the cups are kept, and the sugar. I frown slightly, unwilling to acknowledge that this whole affair may actually have been going on longer than I realized.

'So,' I say brightly, snatching the cups out of Mabel's hands before going to fetch the plates and cutlery myself. I really don't want to know what else she might be familiar with. 'This is nice. Help yourself to breakfast gentlemen.'

By the time the croissants are nearly finished, I know that Jed lives in London and Arnold in Manchester. They are both married. Arnold is on his third. Jed has a teenage boy and Arnold three girls (one for each marriage). And they've not yet met the director of The Bridegroom – someone called David Bollinger, who I'm assured is very well known for his rom coms – or any of the cast due to be filming in Dartmouth.

'Pretty excited actually,' confides Arnold whose previous TV credits include *Manchester Country Life* (I didn't know there was any country life in Manchester), and *Manchester Morgues* (evidently there are a lot of those).

'Had to promise faithfully to bring back autographed photos of Noah Westbrook for all my girls – they'll lynch me if I turn up wi' out 'em.' I laugh with the slightly superior attitude of someone who has already met and been intimately acquainted with the god in question.

'Nope,' interjects Jed, shaking his head, 'my boy's looking for pics of Gaynor Andrews. He thinks she's lovely.' I frown, never having thought to ask who else is in the movie. 'Who is she?' I ask with genuine interest and not a little jealousy (I know, bloody ridiculous). 'I've never heard of her – is she famous?'

'I'll say,' answers Jed whose previous camera skills were tested to the limit on *Celebrity Big Brother*. 'Not in the same league as Noah Westbrook but she was in one o' those reality TV shows a couple o' years back and got spotted by none other than Quentin Tarantino. Apparently, according to those in the know, she's definitely destined for the top. Rumours say her and Noah were once involved. Don't know how true it is though.'

He shifts Dotty, who has been on his lap since he gave her a bit of his croissant, and pushes a slightly creased photograph from his pocket across the table towards me which apparently his teenage son had given him to be signed. Picking up the picture I feel an unavoidable pang of pure envy. Gaynor Andrews is beautiful. I vaguely recognize her from the pages of Hello. Her hair is long, thick, lustrous and of course blond. She has a figure that women like me can only dream about (her hour glass doesn't include a waist of 32 inches).

I am totally unsurprised that she and Noah have been an item, and I can so easily picture the two of them entwined on Noah's pristine white sheets...

'Give us a shufti,' says my father who has been suspiciously quiet for the last half an hour.

I hand over the photograph with a heavy heart and he whistles with complete disregard for the elderly matron sitting next to him.

'Well, she's a looker and no mistake.' Then he looks me up and down, grimaces a bit, reaches across Mabel and promptly removes the last croissant off my plate…

Chapter Eleven

Dotty and I are making our way up through the woods covering the slopes of the Dart Valley behind the house. It's now the middle of the afternoon and I really should be getting myself ready. Kit and Freddy will be coming round in an hour to help me "pretty myself up"...

I think they're on a hiding to nothing myself, but the last time we were together they insisted they had the skills to make me into the bell of the ball – although to be fair, their confidence came after we'd finished the second bottle of plonk...

Finally reaching the top of the valley, Dotty and I sit on a fallen log and survey the whole of the beautiful Dart Valley below. It really is a breathtaking view, but for the first time it doesn't move me the way it does normally. I look down at my scruffy jeans and idly pick off the brambles clinging to my knees.

I turn my attention to Dotty who is now dancing around in an effort to dislodge herself from the leaves stuck to her bottom. Cuddling her to me, I speak out loud. 'Thing is Dotspot, I just wish they'd all quit with the whole Cinderella thing. Between Kit, Freddy and my father, it really is getting completely out of hand. What the hell are they all expecting? If they think we're going to ride off into the sunset together, they better start looking into buying a cart horse.' Unexpectedly the thought of Noah Westbrook trying to fit me behind him on a beautiful white stallion makes me smile. It's all so bloody ridiculous.

And when the hell did I begin to take myself so seriously?

Standing up again, I place Dotty back on the ground and dust myself down. 'Come on Dotspot, let's go and do this,' to which she responds by wagging her tail eagerly and dashing down the trail ahead of me. 'Who needs a prince,' I mutter following her trail. 'The whole fairytale thing is overrated anyway...'

'There is absolutely nothing wrong with making the best of yourself.' Kit stands back to survey her work of art, otherwise known as me... I feel like a bloody fairy on top of a Christmas tree. I am sooo overdressed. Unbeknown to me, my two best friends had conspired to buy me a new outfit.

I am now wearing a fitted (FITTED) sheath dress in black and white with an indecently plunging neckline. (I called it indecent, Kit and Freddy called it making the most of my assets.) Underneath the dress I am wearing what feels like a strait jacket but is, I am reliably informed, invisible smoothing underwear. My hair has been blow dried and curled by Freddy who apparently was a hairdresser in another life. My normally unruly waves are now shiny and smoothly parted on one side and brushed away from my face a la Marilyn Monroe (who, Kit tells me *frequently,* had exactly the same figure as me...)

The whole ensemble is finished off with little black sandals complete with four inch heels and vampy red lipstick.

I look at myself in the mirror. Forget the Christmas tree fairy, I look more like a chunky Cruella Deville. I endeavour to take a deep breath and find that the most I can achieve is a little pant...

'Gorgeous,' breathes Freddy, 'Victory goes to Hollywood. You will stun the whole room my darling.'

'I'll definitely stun someone if I fall off these bloody shoes,' I mutter, staggering around the bedroom to practice. 'I'm not even sure I can sit down.'

'Then stay standing up,' responds Kit unsympathetically. 'Come on Tory, try and get into the whole spirit of the thing. Whatever happens tonight, this will be something for you to look back on and tell your children.' Then, seeing my lack of response at her pep talk, she resorts to handing me a large glass of wine.

Grabbing the glass, I sit gingerly on the edge of the bed and take a deep swallow. 'Are either of you going to be on hand to resuscitate me if I pass out?' Freddy sniggers but I think Kit finally tires of my sarcastic quips. 'Stop being so negative,' she snaps, 'and for God's sake stop bloody whingeing. You've no idea how much I'd love to be in your shoes right now.' I open my mouth to respond then shut it again. I can see that Kit's deadly serious. She's my best friend and I love her. 'I'm so sorry Kitty Kat,' I say softly, 'I really wish it was you going instead of me too.'

'Yeah, well, don't bloody well bugger this up Victory Shackleford. I want to hear every sordid detail when you get back.' Then she walks over and gives me a helping hand up from the bed followed by a quick hug. I feel a lump in the back of my throat. 'And for God's sake don't start crying,' she admonishes, even though her own eyes are suspiciously shiny. 'You'll ruin your mascara.'

'VICTORY 'AVE YOU DONE? I COULD HAVE DRESSED THE WHOLE BLOODY NAVY IN THE TIME IT'S TAKEN YOU TO GET YOUR GLAD RAGS ON.....' My father's bellow from the bottom of the stairs brings an abrupt end to our emotional exchange and Freddy finishes off by saying, 'Amen to that.'

Time to go...

Grabbing my purse and my precious folder of ideas for Noah's house, I turn back to Dotty who is now ensconced in Kit's arms. 'Be a good girl for Aunty Kit,' I murmur, giving her a quick kiss on the head and leaving a bright red lip imprint right between her eyes.

'We'll be waiting,' says Kit, tucking the little dog under her arm. She and Freddy are taking Dotty over the other side to grab some fish and chips, then Kit's going to bunk up in my room for the night. I've drawn the line at Freddy sleeping on the floor, promising faithfully to call him first thing tomorrow.

As I totter slowly down the stairs, I notice that Jed and Arnold are still here and to my blushing delight they enthusiastically wolf whistle as I descend. For once my father doesn't speak, simply nods his head in what I'm assuming is approval as

I reach the bottom. Fortunately he doesn't ask what's in the folder.

'Aren't you two going to the party?' I ask Jed and Arnold who are still standing in their work clothes.

'No such luck Tory,' Arnold responds. 'We'll be working 'til late on this lot here.' He indicates the sound equipment now lying all over the hallway and drawing room floor.

'Don't forget to bring us some Champagne back,' grins Jed wading back into the plethora of seemingly jumbled up wires littering the ground. I frown slightly, really hoping that they don't set the house on fire before we get back...

Ten minutes later Jimmy is driving us up the narrow road to Noah's house. My heart is beginning to thud loudly. Unfortunately there was no opportunity throughout the journey to reinforce my earlier threat to my father (I think that was the main reason dad decided to sit up front with Jimmy – he usually prefers to act as if he's in a limousine...)

And speaking of limousines, just as we arrive at the house, there appears to be one struggling to turn round in front of us. I lean forward (a real challenge in this dress) to see if anyone's getting out. My heart has now moved on to a tango. I'm just praying internally that my father remembers all those important Mess Dinners he attended during his Navy days and acts accordingly...

Once facing back down the hill, the limo in front appears in no hurry to move off, although I can't see anyone actually getting out. After a few minutes my father sighs irritably and indicates that Jimmy should drop us off here. After giving the smaller man strict instructions to 'stand by' for the rest of the evening, dad laboriously climbs out of the front seat and, wonder of wonders, comes round to open the door for me. Then he holds out his hand and helps extract me and my smoothing underwear from the back seat.

Perhaps I have nothing to worry about after all. Early indications appear to suggest that my father intends to be on his best behaviour. I breathe a small sigh of relief as I climb out and take his arm. He definitely looks the part, wearing what the Royal Navy would refer to as "dog robbers" – a smart blazer and trousers together with a sporty little Noel Coward type cravat – all in all the epitome of a retired Admiral.

So far so good...

Arm in arm, we walk towards Noah's house which is still fifty yards away. It's a beautiful evening. Despite the hour, the sun is glinting warmly through the trees and what sounds like the entire local bird population is chattering away in a flurry of spring nest building.

As we get closer to the still stationary limousine, the driver door suddenly opens and out springs an immaculately groomed chauffeur. Full of avid curiosity, we slow our steps to avoid arriving at the car at the exact same time as he throws open the rear passenger door. After a couple of seconds, a long tanned leg languorously unfolds from the opening together with a perfectly manicured hand, imperiously requesting the chauffeur's assistance. Dad and I glance at each other, and grin, for once in complete accord. This has got to be someone famous. Stopping completely about ten yards from the limo, we wait in a fever of anticipation to see who gets out.

A couple of minutes later, we're not disappointed. The vision extracting herself from the car is none other than Gaynor Andrews. She's absolutely breathtaking. Every movement as she straightens up and then gracefully reaches back into the car for her purse seems to be perfectly choreographed. She's wearing a pure white jumpsuit that clings to every curve. The front is low-cut, revealing a subtle, tantalizing glimpse of her small, perfectly formed breasts.

Self consciously I let go of my father's arm, and tug on my own plunging neckline reflecting that my dress is definitely not subtle anything. My father, for once completely speechless, doesn't even notice I've dropped his arm, and is continuing to stare, open mouthed, at the beautiful woman in front of him. Her ensemble is completed by silver strappy, impossibly high heels, which she doesn't have any problem walking elegantly in.

Without acknowledging the chauffeur, she steps aside gracefully as he shuts the car door, then notices us for the first time. Frowning slightly, she lifts her Dior sunglasses and regards us in much the way I imagine a cat would stare at a mouse. After a couple of seconds, no doubt thinking us of absolutely no note whatsoever, she replaces the sunglasses on her petite nose and turns away without bothering to speak. I am astonished at her blatant rudeness and hold my breath, fully expecting my father to tear a strip off the actress in his usual abrupt manner. However, he simply stares after her like a love struck puppy, then looks back down at me with a sparkle in his eyes.

'This is the life, Victory.' My heart stutters and sinks at the eager glint in his eyes. 'Takes me back to that dinner I had with The Queen. Had 'er Majesty rolling in the aisles,' he confided in a theatrical whisper. 'Don't you worry my girl, I know how to rub shoulders with the rich and famous. I'll have 'em all in stitches in no time...'

I need alcohol!

Taking a deep breath (or as deep as this damn dress will allow), I hold dad back a little, really not wanting to catch up to the leading lady at Noah's front door. I have never in my whole life felt so much out of my depth. I can't imagine what I was thinking in wanting to come here. I should have made an excuse. Any excuse. Pulling at my father's arm, I attempt to get his attention, intending to inform him that I really don't feel well (definitely not a lie) and want to go home. However, before I get chance to open my mouth, our host catches sight of us hovering in the road and, extracting himself from Gaynor Andrews' enthusiastic embrace, walks towards us with a smile.

'Hey guys, so glad you made it.' His greeting is friendly and open, as though he's genuinely glad to see us. Out of the corner of my eye, I can see the actress still standing in the doorway. Sunglasses off, she is staring back at us, no doubt wondering if we're the hired help...

I turn my attention back to Noah who is shaking my father's

hand and clapping him on the back. Wearing a simple white shirt and stone coloured jeans, he looks good enough to eat, and as he turns those heavy lidded, oh so sexy, blue eyes on to me I feel the blush begin at my toes and work its way up…

'You look gorgeous Tory.' His eyes are warm and the blush turns into crimson heat. I know he's just being kind, but it's not every day one gets told that she looks gorgeous by a Hollywood sex symbol. Struggling for a suitably gracious response, I end up simply holding out my folder. 'I've brought your drawings,' is my amazing, super cool attempt at flirtation.

'That's great. Maybe we can find some time later to go over them.'

'Like the bedroom?' I want to say, but luckily it comes out as , 'Err, sure, that would be good.' My father is looking back and forward between us during the exchange with a look of bewildered delight on his face and I remember that he doesn't know anything about my earlier visit. Fortunately, for once in his life, he says nothing and allows Noah to guide us back towards the house.

Gaynor Andrews is no longer standing on the front porch and I get the feeling that she doesn't do waiting. Once inside the beautiful hallway, I'm careful to show the same amazement as earlier and simply follow Noah through into the drawing room towards the sound of talking and laughter. As we enter the room, curious glances are sent our way and it is very obvious that we are the only two strangers in the room, apart from the waiters carrying around trays of canapés and Champagne.

'Hey everyone. Meet Admiral Charles Shackleford and his daughter Tory. These are the guys who have been kind enough to loan us their house to film in.'

There is a small silence where I sense us being looked up and down en mass by Noah's guests – I get the distinct feeling it's mostly down. Then, as the quiet lengthens, my father clears his throat and steps forward, causing my heart to judder in horrified anticipation.

'It's very nice to meet you all.' I let out the breath I didn't know

I was holding and smile weakly, even going so far as to give a little half wave to the assembly.

'So where does a man get a drink around here. The inside of my mouth feels like a Swahili witch doctor's shammy leather ju ju bag...'

My father has never even heard of political correctness.

An hour later I am nursing my third glass of Champagne while propping up the wall. My embarrassment at my father's social gaff has dulled to resentment. It seems that my rude, unpredictable, politically incorrect old man is a hit with the Hollywood locals. I can hear them all roaring with laughter as my father describes with relish the antics of an old junior rating whose nickname had apparently been Whacker Payne on account that (a) His name was Payne and (b) he was (and I quote) 'rigged like a Nagasaki donkey'

But slowly, as I listen to my father enthusiastically recounting some of his more daring naval exploits (and by daring I think he's generally referring to those adventures resulting from alcoholic over indulgence), I really can't help but smile and I realise that actually it's not always necessary to fit in. My father has spent his whole life as a testament to that. He has never, to my knowledge, toed the line and he's all the happier for it.

Okay, so perhaps his constant flouting of convention has pushed me to the other extreme, but I can't spend the rest of my life blaming everything on dad and it really is time I loosened up a little. I take a deep breath followed by another gulp of my Champagne and, placing my precious drawings carefully on a small side table, I head over to the buffet table and small talk...

'So there I was dahling, simply dying of boredom when along comes this absolutely divine young man to sweep me off my feet, and I've never really looked back.' I position myself between a very mature British lady who sort of resembles a praying mantis and an ageing American gentleman with an impressive pot belly and huge mutton chop whiskers. I have no idea who they are but assume that the American at least is an actor – nobody would voluntarily sport facial hair directly out of an episode of Downton Abbey if not in preparation for a part in The Bridegroom. Unsure whether to interrupt or not, I stand and fidget self consciously while listening to their conversation, which appears to be centred around the merits of having a younger partner – of the type recommended by Joan Collins...

I'm just beginning to wonder whether I may have picked the wrong conversation to begin my loosening up efforts when I suddenly realize that I have become the object of their discussion. The elderly actress is staring at me expectantly while mutton chops is leering down the front of my dress very unattractively (I'm going to kill Kit). I glance from one to the other wondering if I've just been propositioned by someone old enough to be my grandfather and whether there are any normal people here I can talk to. I stall for time, 'Don't even go there you disgusting old lecher,' is not likely to cut the mustard, no matter which way you look at it.

'Hey Tory, so good to meet you,' comes a pleasant male voice at my back. 'I really can't wait to start filming in your fabulous house.' I swing round gratefully and come face to face with a youngish sandy haired man holding out his hand towards me. 'David Bollinger, I'm the director of The Bridegroom for my sins.' His smile is boyish and mischievous, telling me clearly that he has overheard the conversation. 'Have these two old reprobates introduced themselves to you yet?' he continues, waving towards the two fossils behind me.

His smile is definitely infectious and I relax and grin back as I shake my head. 'How insufferably rude and un-English like – Patsy, I thought better of you at least.' His tone is light and slightly mocking but there is steel underneath that makes clear his dislike of boorish behaviour.

'Tory, this is Patsy Mallon and Donald Peterson. They are both veterans of stage and screen and we're all very grateful to have them amongst the cast in The Bridegroom. Patsy is pure delight as Lady Eva Trentham and Donald is perfectly cast as the evil, scheming Marquis of Rutland.'

I smile and nod towards the two actors like I know exactly

what he's talking about. Why haven't I made an effort to find out exactly what the bloody movie's about? I know it's a romantic comedy but that's about the sum of my knowledge. Sometimes I totally despair of myself. The thing is, nobody's actually asked me. All I know is rom coms are not usually my thing. I resolve to do some research the minute I get home.

'How long are you going to be filming in Dartmouth?' I ask to forestall any more discussion about the movie's plot.

'We're booked in to the Dart Marina hotel for three and a half weeks and your father has very kindly given us carte blanche with the Admiralty for four. Obviously I'm hoping to wrap filming up as soon as possible. You know the old adage time is money? Well in this case it's most definitely true.' He pauses to take a sip of Champagne. 'Having said that, it takes as long as it takes. You never know, we might even be joining you for Thanksgiving.' He smiles and, unbidden, the image of Noah Westbrook joining us for Christmas dinner pops into my head, surprising me with its intensity.

'Have you got the whole cast staying in Dartmouth?' I ask, shoving the school girl fantasy firmly back where it belongs.

'No, only those needed for the scenes being filmed on location here. Let's see, there's Noah who, as you know, is the Bridegroom of the title and Gaynor Andrews who plays an American heiress and his love interest; Patsy and Donald are the villains of the piece and over near the patio doors are Luke Smitherd, Gina Sheridan, Amy Winters, Jack Taylor and Scott Davies, all playing members of the Collingwood family who are staying in Devon for a weekend house party, which of course is performed beautifully by your house'

I look over at the small group who seem vaguely familiar and nod my head, feeling the excitement rise at being surrounded by so many household names (well, stands to reason they must be names in some people's houses.) I take a sip of my wine. 'It's really very thrilling' (thrilling, where did that come from...?) But the thing is, I actually mean it. 'Will it be okay to watch you filming?' I ask hopefully.

'Outside, no problem at all. Inside might be a little trickier. You're gonna have to live in your kitchen for the next two weeks while we commandeer your hall and living room.' He smiles again, taking the sting out of the command.

'No worries,' I quip back, 'I can sleep on a mattress near the stove – I've been told I make a good Cinderella.'

'A little on the fat side for a convincing Cinders aren't you darling?' Gaynor Andrews appears in a cloud of Chanel at my shoulder and raises her eyebrows to Patsy and Donald who chuckle into their drinks at her comment.

I feel my face flame at her spitefulness while my mind tries to come up with something witty and cutting to say back. Unfortunately I'm not in the same league as my father at snide comebacks and I stay humiliatingly silent. David doesn't say anything but his look towards the actress is anything but friendly, which makes me feel a bit better.

'Not everyone spends their whole life eating celery and laxative chocolate, Gay.' Noah's voice as he appears at my other shoulder, is equally cutting, and his face, when I look up at him, is hard and closed.

I glance between him and Gaynor Andrews, sensing old undercurrents. There is a brief silence, then the actress lets out a tinkling laugh, 'Don't be such an old grouch sweetie,' she admonishes Noah. 'Tory knows I was only funning, don't you darling?' The last is directed to me and I have no idea how to answer. 'Come on baby, don't be cross.' Her voice continues in a soft, intimate southern drawl and I feel her hand reaching out behind my back to stroke Noah's arm in a reconciliatory gesture. This is the big league and I'm so not equipped to deal with it.

'Well now, I'd hazard a guess that everything you know about the subject of my daughter could be written on the outside of a gnat's bollock bag…'

My father's loud rebuke creates an instant of incredulous silence followed by a few furtive chuckles, hurriedly turned into coughs. Gaynor Andrews glances round as if she can't believe anyone could possibly speak to her that way. The geriatric twosome titter into their glasses again and I just want to give the pair of them a sharp slap.

Taking a deep breath, the actress glares back at my father with icy hauteur, which of course, is absolutely water off a duck's back to the Admiral. I can tell she's gearing herself up for a biting comeback and I actually feel sorry for her. The last time anyone bested my father in a slanging match was when he was a sub-lieutenant over forty years ago. Wincing, I shut my eyes, waiting for the inevitable…

…Which thankfully never arrives. Noah, possibly after looking at my panic stricken face, diffuses the situation by saying in an amused dry voice, 'The Admiral's only funning Gay; you know that don't you sweetheart?' Despite his tongue in cheek repetition of Gaynor's earlier comment, my gut clenches in jealousy at his use of the endearment. His words are soft and intimate, in marked contrast to his earlier cutting tone, and are enough to diffuse the tension. Glancing up at the actress, I intercept a hungry, almost desperate look towards Noah and I realize in that instant that the rumours about the two of them are obviously true, and, if they are no longer together, then it's not of Gaynor Andrews' doing.

If Noah's aware of Gaynor's feelings, he gives no sign and appears to be oblivious to her look of longing as he directs the hired staff to bring round more Champagne and canapés. As the waiter approaches, he turns towards me, takes my now empty glass and replaces it with a full one from the tray before taking one for himself. Then, to my amazement, he suggests we take our drinks into the study to have a look at my drawings.

Noah excuses us both with the joke that he's taking me to look at his etchings. I avoid looking at Gaynor as I pick up my drawings and we weave our way across the room, but as Noah opens the door to the study, I glance back to see her watching us with a blank expression.

As I turn back to the door, I catch sight of my father who is also watching us. But instead of an unsmiling poker face, he offers a lewd wink and the thumbs up sign.

I don't know which scares me most...

Once in the study, Noah closes the door to shut out the noise of conversation. 'Won't your guests think you're rude abandoning them like this?' I can't help but ask.

Without looking up, Noah places his Champagne glass on to a small side table. 'They won't even notice we've gone,' is all he says dismissively as he takes the folder out of my hand. I don't know what else to say and resort to sipping my drink in silence as he opens the folder and spreads the drawings on a large mahogany desk. The silence lengthens and I can't help but fiddle with my glass as anxiety sets in. Dipping my finger in the liquid, I idly run its wet tip around the rim of the glass, creating a loud whining sound after a few seconds.

'Didn't your parents ever tell you it's rude to fidget?' Noah says eventually without lifting his head from the drawings in front of him.

'Sorry,' I mumble, taking a large gulp of my drink instead.

After what feels like ten hours but is actually only ten minutes, Noah finally looks up. His face is unreadable and my heart sinks, expecting him to say that my ideas are not what he's looking for. Then, leaning back against the edge of the table, he folds his arms and half closes his eyes. After a couple of minutes he straightens up. 'I've made an offer on the house which has been accepted, he says without preamble. 'You can start the work as soon as there's a suitable gap in your calendar.'

I gape at him momentarily. It is so not what I was expecting him to say. Then my heart begins to pound and I want to rush over and hug him. 'Thank you so much,' I breathe finally with a big smile. 'You won't regret this Noah, I promise you. Of course we'll have to get an architect in for the outside alterations, and a reputable builder; that's before we even think about the inside.' Feverishly I take out my notebook and start scribbling, completely lost in another world.

'I'll leave all the finer details to you,' he continues while I'm writing. 'You can contact me on the cell number I gave you – at least while I'm still in Dartmouth. Once filming's finished,

I'll give you another number. In the meantime, if you'll give me your bank account details, I'll have some money transferred into your account. How much do you want? Will a hundred grand be enough to start you off?'

Once again I look at him with my mouth open. He grins at me before saying, 'That really isn't your most attractive look Tory, which causes me to shut my mouth again with a snap, and him to laugh. 'When do you think you'll be starting the project?' he continues, still smiling. 'It'd be good if we can at least make a start while I'm still here, but no pressure.'

'That shouldn't be a problem.' My voice comes out in a high squeak and I cough self consciously. 'I have about three properties on the go at the moment but they're all nearing completion, so I'll begin checking to see which architects and builders are available as soon as I get home.'

'I don't think it's necessary for you to start tonight.' His voice is now teasing and warm and I have absolutely no idea what to say back. No witty response comes to mind at all. My mind is a complete blank.

'No, of course not, I just want... I mean I would just like... I mean, I really will do a good job – I promise.' Hurriedly I look back down at my notes, very aware I'm now babbling - again.

'I know you will Tory. I trust you completely.' The way he says my name does weird things to my groin area and I look up uncertainly to find him lounging against the desk, hands in his pockets, regarding me intently. The smile is gone, replaced by a serious searching expression, as if he can't quite fathom me out. Which is ridiculous – I'm about as transparent as they come.

'I err, I, well I err, umm, I think that's about it for tonight then.' I stammer finally when he doesn't say anything. I can feel the excitement bubbling up inside me - so strong that I want to punch the air and shout woo hoo at the top of my voice. Instead, apart from a broad smile which I couldn't suppress if my life depended on, I try for dignified and professional and, stepping forward, I hold out my hand to shake his.

After a split second, he pushes himself off the desk, the

intense look replaced with an answering smile. Just as we're about to shake hands on the deal, my oh so ridiculous heels finally let me down and I stumble forward with a shriek, my outstretched hand now flailing in the air as I try to keep my balance. In the end, gravity wins and I fall into Noah's arms with an awkward oomph, causing him to grunt slightly as he takes my full weight and falls back against the edge of the desk.

My face ends up in the crook of his neck and for a second I breathe in his wonderful scent before pure humiliation sets in. Damn it, every time we're together, I seem to end up in some kind of embarrassing position. Face flaming, I push myself away from his chest and look up to his face, expecting to see irritation if not downright annoyance. Instead, astonishingly, as I stare up into his incredible eyes, all I can see is hunger.

My heart begins to beat in a quick staccato rhythm in response to their midnight intensity, then all thought flees and pure sensation takes over as he bends his head and kisses me. I know I should pull away, no good can possibly come from this, but, instead and purely instinctively, I part my lips under his onslaught and immediately his tongue darts in to tangle with mine in a way that turns my insides to liquid fire.

Time seems to stand still as I force down the small voice of reason and surrender totally to the heat coursing around my body. Somehow my hands find their way around the back of his neck to tangle in his hair and Noah groans in response, deepening his kiss.

His hands are moulding me to him, pressing me against the hard length of him and I feel the last of my control slipping away. I don't care where this goes; I want this, I want *him*, now...

Then suddenly, shockingly, there's a loud knock on the door. Panting, I pull away from Noah's arms, the cold light of reality swamping me like a bucket of cold water being dashed over my head. Stumbling back, I tear my eyes away from his glittering gaze and look towards the door which is now being pushed open hesitantly.

'Hope I'm not disturbing anything,' come the mild tones of

David Bollinger as his head appears around the slowly opening door.

I don't trust myself to speak. My heart is still thumping erratically in my chest and all I can think is 'Oh my God, what have I done?'

I look back over to Noah. His face is completely expressionless and his body language relaxed, giving no indication at all that two minutes ago, he was kissing me like he wanted to fit me inside of his skin.

'You're not interrupting anything David. We were just finishing up here.' Then glancing towards me, he continues, 'You got everything Tory? Just give me a call if you need me – although I guess we'll almost be living together over the next couple of weeks.' His smile is friendly, but nothing more.

The kiss didn't mean anything to him. I was just a distraction. And why on earth would I possibly think it meant anything more...?

Taking a deep breath, I smile brightly back, trying to ignore my still unsteady pulse. 'I don't need anything else for now. You can keep the drawings; I have copies.' Then, fighting the urge to cry, I lift my head, square my shoulders and walk over to the door. David is still hovering in the doorway; he smiles at me without speaking, and moves aside to let me pass.

Glancing around the drawing room, I immediately notice two things: firstly, that Gaynor Andrews is not there, and secondly, my father is completely surrounded by the on screen members of the Collingwood family. Breathing a sigh of relief, I walk straight over to the buffet table and load up my plate with as many delicious canapés as it will hold, then, turning to an opened bottle of Champagne nestling in a bucket of ice, I pick up the bucket...

Saturday 10th May

TO: kim@kimberleyharris.com

Hey Kimmy

Sitting with a Scotch before turning in and thought I'd just send you a quick update. You'll be glad to know that my little soiree went without a hitch. All the usual suspects were there and it was pretty much same old, same old – not being around them for a while, I forgot how much bullshit they all talk! Gaynor unfortunately decided to grace us with her presence and was a royal pain in the ass as usual. For some reason she seemed to take an instant dislike to Tory (you remember, the Admiral's daughter – told you I was inviting them right?) Anyway, she made some snipey comments about Tory being fat. God, she was so bloody rude sis. But you know the funny thing is, until Gaynor said that, I'd not really paid much attention. But when you really look at her, Tory's actually kinda pretty – especially when she smiles, and you have no idea just how refreshing it is to see a woman who does not look like a stick insect :-) Anyhow, I managed to smooth everything before Gaynor drew blood and think she left pretty soon after.

And as for the Admiral - the old man really is absolutely nuts; I gave him a vintage bottle of port as a gift for having us all mess up his back yard and he actually drank most of it before he left last night– but not before he treated us all to half a dozen sea shanties which he insisted we all sing along to, even had David joining in. I could still hear him singing as Tory helped him out to the car at one am. What a guy…

Anyhow, think you might well get to meet him seeing as the offer I made for the house was accepted, so I'm gonna be round and about. I know you'll all love it here. I've asked Tory to project manage the alterations. Hoping she can make a start while I'm still here filming.

So that's my news sis. Give my love to Ben and the kids, speak soon

Noah

xxx

Chapter Twelve

Sunday was cloudy and windy which suited Admiral Shackleford's mood entirely. His head felt like the inside of a Viking's leather truss after consuming almost an entire bottle of top notch ten year old port at the end of the evening. He didn't really remember Tory getting him home but assumed Jimmy had a hand in it somewhere. Still, hair of the dog and all that – a pint of the Ship Inn's Special Bitter would do the business.

By the time he pushed open the pub door, most of the Sunday lunchtime rush has been and gone. The interior was welcomingly quiet and dim, and the air redolent with the fading aroma of roast beef. He sniffed appreciatively and wondered if they'd have enough beef left to put him a quick sarnie together. Didn't have time for the whole shebang as he'd asked Mabel to come over for dinner, promising to take her over to the Pictures in Paignton afterwards and he definitely needed to get his head down before that if he wasn't to fall asleep on the back row.

A few minutes later, he was tucking into a doorstep beef sandwich complete with a leftover Yorkshire pudding and gravy just as a windswept Jimmy pushed open the door. Pickles had his own little bowl of scraps at the Admiral's feet.

'Can't stop long sir,' the small man said breathlessly as he trotted over to the bar. 'Emily's just popped over the other side to M&S before it closes so I've got about half an hour 'til she's back. The kids are coming over for dinner tonight so I've got to move the best china.'

The Admiral looked irritably at his friend over the top of his sandwich. 'Don't know how you cope with all those carpet crawlers of yours. How many are there now – twenty or something?'

Jimmy chuckled, completely unfazed by the Admiral's description of his grandchildren. 'Just four sir, although I admit, it does sometimes feel like there's a lot more of 'em.'

'Humph,' was all the Admiral responded. Jimmy secretly thought that his old commanding officer had a private longing for a couple of his own carpet crawlers, but of course he never said anything.

'How are you feeling today sir?' he asked instead, having witnessed (and participated in) the long and arduous task of getting the well oiled Admiral to bed the night before. He and Tory had taken an arm each as they helped him from the car, into the house and up the stairs. Everything had been going ship-shape until they began staggering up the staircase, where the operation could well have proved fatal on several occasions due to the Admiral's continual attempts to wave his arms around in time to his own unique and very loud interpretation of "Life on the Ocean Wave".

The whole undertaking was made all the more hazardous, not to mention deafening, as both Dotty and Pickles added their enthusiastic barking while darting up and down the stairs with complete disregard to the fact that it was one thirty in the morning.

The Admiral sighed at Jimmy's probing before admitting that 'He'd felt better,' prior to ordering another pint. They went on to sit in companionable silence for a couple of minutes. The only noise that could be heard was Pickles knocking his bowl around the room in an attempt to get the last of the gravy stuck round the outside.

At length, the Admiral turned to his oldest friend and said, 'Think we are cooking on gas Jimmy my boy. The package seemed mighty interested in our Victory – even disappearing off with her into his study for a full half hour.' He frowned as a sudden thought occurred to him. 'Hope he's not tampering with the goods though.'

'Oh I'm sure Tory isn't that kind of girl Sir, she wouldn't even consider letting someone she's only just met into her locker.'

'Mmm,' was the Admiral's only response, either indicating that he didn't share Jimmy's faith in his daughter's moral standards, or that Victory would be completely incapable of resisting someone of Noah Westbrook's sex appeal. Probably a bit of both...

'Well, I'm not taking any chances with our Victory's reputation. I'll be keeping a close watch on the package over the next couple of weeks. Make no mistake Jimmy, it's wedding bells I'm looking for and I'll not accept anything less for my only daughter...'

Chapter Thirteen

Despite the fact that it was gone two o'clock by the time I went to bed last night, I'm awake bright and early. Well, in all honesty, I'm not that bright given that I did consume the better part of a bottle of Champagne last night – or was it two? My head has been pounding for the last hour, giving a strong indication it might have been the latter.

As I lie there listening to Kit's deep breathing and Dotty's occasional dreaming twitch, I go over the events of the evening in my head for the umpteenth time. Kit was awake when I got home last night, (how could she not be after the racket we made?) For some reason though, I didn't tell her about Noah's kiss. I'm not sure why. I think maybe I'm afraid she'll make too much of it and the only way that route will end is in tears. He's famous *and* drop dead gorgeous, totally used to women throwing themselves at him (in my case, literally). He was most likely just curious as to what it felt like to grope someone who was larger than the average Hollywood stick insect.

I told her all about Noah's amazing job offer though and bless her, she was excited as me. I spent another hour droning on about his house and my ideas for updating it and she didn't drop off once, although that could have been more because Dotty's snoring at one point was loud enough to wake the dead. Climbing quietly out of bed, I resolve to put the whole kiss incident right out of my mind and concentrate on the important stuff – like taking some pain killers for this bloody headache.

An hour later Kit and I are legging it down the garden in an attempt to catch the car ferry waiting at the slip. Although it's Sunday, I'm eager to make a start on Noah's project as soon as possible, so while Kit opens the gallery to tourists, I intend to hole up in the back office and get cracking.

We make it to the ferry with seconds to spare and as I look back towards the Admiralty, I can see figures beginning to swarm around the garden. The house had already been filling up with the film crew as we left and I only managed a quick wave to Arnold and Jed who appeared to be tied up with the big boys of the operation.

My decision to head to the gallery to work was definitely the right one.

By lunchtime I've sent emails to a reputable builder and an architect in Torquay who I've worked with before. Both are trustworthy and have an amazing ability to think outside the box – not always a given in south Devon. So far, I haven't mentioned who the client is because (a) I can't trust them not to shout it from the rooftops and (b) I don't want Noah to be ripped off. I know, I know, he has plenty of dosh but that's not the point.

After pressing send on the last email, I decide to pop out to grab a bite to eat and give Dotty a chance to do her business. The gallery is very busy as I pass through and I make a discreet chomping motion to Kit as I head for the door, asking if she wants me to bring her a sandwich. At her nod, I give her a quick thumbs up and walk out into the fresh air, which today is cloudy and windy with a hint of rain. What a difference a day makes I reflect, pulling my cardigan across my chest. Dotty loves this kind of weather though and trots happily along with her nose in the air, appreciatively sniffing the wonderful smells carried on the salty air.

After buying two wraps from the local deli, I walk over to the small park in the centre of Dartmouth and we take a seat near the bandstand. Despite, or perhaps because of, the inclement weather, the town is buzzing. A yachting and tourist haven both,

Dartmouth always has its fair share of visitors, but today there seem to be more people around than usual. I wonder how many are here hoping for a glimpse of the cast of The Bridegroom. I sit eating my sandwich while I people watch.

Dotty is curled up on the bench with her head in my lap gazing up at me in her ever hopeful, feed me, I'm starving, mode. Finishing my wrap, I look down to give her the last bit when suddenly she jumps off the bench, barking ecstatically as a tall figure walks over and stops in front of me, blocking out my light. With a sense of déjà vu, I squint upwards to see a tall man wearing glasses and a beany hat. Despite the disguise, I know who it is instantly, as does Dotty who is now making excited little whimpering noises as she attempts to climb up his leg.

'Shouldn't you be hard at work creating me the house of my dreams?' he says mildly, and sits down beside me. 'Shouldn't you be hard at it earning enough money to pay me?' I respond flippantly, despite my heart hammering ten to the dozen, so loudly he can probably hear it. Dotty is beside herself with delight and is now wriggling blissfully all over his lap in an effort to lick any part of him that's uncovered. I watch her with envy - if only I could do the same...

'They're busy backing my trailer into your yard as we speak,' he counters, waving vaguely in the direction of the river. 'Unfortunately, as you can no doubt imagine, the angle means it's not exactly an easy feat, particularly if we don't want it to finish up floating in the Dart after creating a long swathe of destruction through your newly immaculate flower beds.'

'What do you mean, newly immaculate?' I grin, despite myself. The garden was most definitely my mother's domain; dad and I wouldn't know the difference between a dahlia and a dandelion. He smiles back and asks if I have time to join him for a cup of tea. Instead of giving in to the impulse to shove Dotty off and throw myself into his lap, I sigh dramatically and tell him I can spare fifteen minutes before I have to get back to the grindstone. 'But first I have to take my friend Kit her lunch.' I hold up the extra wrap for him to see. 'She doesn't have my padding and will very likely starve to death if I don't feed her at regular intervals.'

Standing up, I brush the crumbs off my knees and lift Dotty off his lap, ignoring her grumble of protest – I think she was settling in for the day. 'Do you want to come with me or shall I meet you somewhere?' He gets to his feet and waves at me to go on in front. 'Lead on fair maiden; I would in faith be honoured to be introduced to those you call friends.'

I am torn between wanting to introduce Kit because I know how much it will mean to her, and selfish reluctance because – well, to put it simply, she's so much prettier than me. 'Don't be so bloody ridiculous you silly vain twit,' I reprimand myself crossly as we head back towards the gallery.

I don't know whether to be happy or sad that the gallery is now empty as I lead Noah through the door. I call out to Kit as he glances around the exhibits with interest and after a couple of seconds, she comes through from the back where she's been making a hot drink.

'OMG, I'm so glad of five minutes peace. I might just strangle the next bloody tourist who walks through that door. Did you bring me some gr…?' She stops in mid grumble, as, like me, she instantly recognizes the tall lithe figure of Noah Westbrook standing behind me. I can't stop the stab of jealousy that rips through me as I notice for the first time today the tight jeans and skimpy tank top she's wearing.

As she continues to gawp at the actor, I step forward to make the introductions. 'This is my best friend Kit Davies. Kit, this is Noah Westbrook. I don't think I need to tell you who he is…' I hope my lack of enthusiasm isn't too obvious in my voice, but to be honest, I don't think Kit would've noticed if I'd introduced her as the Whore of Babylon. As soon as I began speaking, she went completely and totally uncharacteristically red. Like a beetroot. I completely forget my doubts as I stare at her in fascination. I really can't remember the last time Kit didn't have a lightening quick retort. Obviously used to this kind of response, Noah steps forward and holds out his hand. 'Hey, it's great to meet you Kit.' His voice, as always, is open and friendly and shakes Kit out of her inertia.

'Yes,' is her earth shattering response. Noah raises his eyebrows a little and I resist the urge to snigger at my usually cool as a cucumber best friend.

Just then, the gallery door opens to admit a group of five pensioners and Kit immediately snaps to. Apparently the over seventies in general cause more damage to enormously expensive works of art than a classroom full of ten year olds. And, although it clearly states that all breakages must be paid for, the chances of getting your average aurally challenged eighty year old to cough up are slim to none. In fact you'd probably have more luck with the ten year old. At least the dangerous bags they're swinging around have a tendency to contain a bit more than a couple of fluff covered mint humbugs and a purse that needs a fifteen digit code to access.

As Kit goes into KGB mode, I hurriedly usher Noah into the office at the back. Dotty is already ensconced in her basket. Looking back at the gaggle of elderly ladies oohing and aahing over a beautiful (and unique) two thousand pound china clock, I estimate that none of them are likely to see eighty five again. My observation is endorsed by Kit's white face as she positions herself close enough to catch the rare timepiece should the need arise. I realize we are not going to get past them any time soon – not without serious repercussions to both ageing hearts and costly artifacts – both obviously irreplaceable...

So I ask Noah if he'd like a cup of tea here instead. 'Yeah, that'd be great,' is his easy response and, shrugging off his lightweight navy jacket, he makes himself comfortable on one of the ancient easy chairs as I bustle about like an honorary member of the Waltons. As he sits down, Dotty promptly jumps up on to his knee and settles down. She closes her eyes with a contented sigh, then rapidly opens them again as she hears me unearth a packet of biscuits. There wasn't even a tell tale rustle, but I'm not surprised. Past experience has shown that her nose is more than capable of sniffing out a ginger nut half a mile away.

Is a mug ok?' I ask, unsure of what I'll do if he says no, as it's pretty much a mug or nothing. 'Super,' he grins back with an exaggerated English accent.

As I hand him his tea, I note he's taken off his hat, which has left his hair all tousled and oh so yummy. The glasses are still on, so he actually looks like a sexy boffin. I'm doomed. Swallowing, I quickly turn back to the plate of biscuits. 'Ginger nut?' I ask, thrusting the plate under his nose. He blinks and rears back slightly in an effort to avoid inhaling one, then gingerly (pardon the pun) takes one off the plate, examines it and sniffs it. 'Ginger,' he confirms with a half smile. 'Never had one of these before. Why do you call it a nut when it's clearly a biscuit?'

I am nonplussed and have to confess I have absolutely no idea. I seat myself in the other, even shabbier chair and watch him take a bite of his biscuit. 'Bloody hell that's hard,' he says as he finally gets his teeth through the exterior. 'Maybe that's why they call it a nut,' I tease smiling. 'Of course, we haven't all got your sensitive Hollywood teeth, but, actually, there's an art to eating a ginger biscuit. Watch and learn...' With exaggerated care, I dunk my biscuit into my tea. 'The key is not to leave it in so long that it disintegrates into your drink, but just long enough to soften the outside.' Taking a bite I close my eyes and sigh with pleasure, allowing the biscuit to melt on my tongue while savouring the ginger essence. It really is the little things...

Then I look over at him intending to say, 'Your turn,' only to find him staring at me. Or more specifically, my mouth. Silence. 'Err, have I got crumbs?' I say eventually, self consciously brushing my fingers over my lips. 'No, no crumbs,' he answers absently, still staring at me. I try to come up with another witty comment, but my stock of sarcastic quips seems to have dried up. 'Would you like another?' is all I come up with in the end. Blinking, he comes back from wherever he's been and looks down at the half eaten biscuit still in his hand. 'Better not rush things,' he says finally in mock seriousness. 'The loss of half a biscuit is better than a whole one. I'm going in...'

I laugh again and the weird tension is broken. 'Perfect,' he says a couple of seconds later after popping the soggy remainder into his mouth. 'Yep, I'll have another one.' He glances down at Dotty, who, having jumped off his knee at the prospect of biscuits, has now resorted to doing a war dance around his trouser leg. 'And I think she wants one too.'

A few minutes later, Kit comes back into the office and, seeing both chairs taken, wearily lowers herself into Dotty's basket. 'My nerves are completely shot,' she says without preamble. 'I'm seriously thinking of banning everyone over the age of sixty five unless they leave their handbags at the door.'

'Tea?' I ask after checking my watch and thinking maybe it's still a little too early for anything stronger. 'You're an angel,' she responds with a sigh, then reading my mind, 'Have we got any whisky to put in it?'

'Don't think so.' I climb out of my chair to investigate and wave towards the vacated seat. 'Sit down sweetie, you still look as white as a sheet.' Then, walking over to an alcove in the back of the room, I throw open the doors of an old filing cabinet which houses both of our accounts. Shoving the jumbled up papers out of the way, (I know, I know, and to make it worse, we both use the same accountant – she's currently in therapy), I manage to unearth a dusty bottle. 'There's still some of that alcoholic mouth wash your Polish ex brought you back from Krakow,' I shout with my head still in the cupboard.

'Oh my God, am I that desperate?' muses Kit, who still hasn't moved from Dotty's bed. 'Yep, I think so. Bring it on…'

I carry the bottle back over to the table holding the tea making paraphernalia and the rest of the mugs – some of which I'm ashamed to note have possibly a new strain of penicillin growing inside - and switch the kettle back on. Next, pulling the cork out with my teeth, I add a generous measure of what apparently passes in Poland for a top notch liqueur (it really does taste like that pink stuff they give you to swill your mouth out at the dentists) and add a tea bag and some milk which immediately curdles ominously. 'Just waiting for the kettle,' I say, giving it a quick stir.

As Kit finally makes an effort to extract herself from the

basket, Noah jumps up to help.

Bloody hell, for a second I'd forgotten he was there. It's scary the way he just seems to fit in, wherever he is. I watch with envy the ease with which he pulls up her tiny frame then glance down at the vacated basket. I couldn't even fit my right buttock in it.

Kit is now blushing prettily again as she murmurs, 'Thank you,' and sits herself down in the empty chair. Sighing, I bring over the murky looking liquid that could, in an extremely dark room, pass for tea. She takes a large sip then pulls a face. 'Oh my God that is truly disgusting.'

'Then fear not fair lady, Dr Freddy is here with the perfect cure for all your ills. Along with a corkscrew.'

I turn towards the office door to see Freddy leaning nonchalantly against the frame holding a bottle of red wine triumphantly in the air. 'You can thank me later peeps. Just point me towards three glasses.' Then, noticing Noah for the first time and without missing a beat, 'Make that four.'

My heart sinks just a little at Freddy's arrival, no doubt because I forgot to call him this morning. It's not that I don't love him - he's my second best friend – but he can be a bit of an acquired taste, and I've no idea what Noah will make of him...

I needn't have worried, the actor's manners are, as always, impeccable and he immediately stands up as I make the introductions. Stepping forward to shake Noah's proffered hand, Freddy lets slip a small nervous laugh, but on the whole, holds it together admirably. I'm the only one who can see his other hand trembling slightly as he hands me the bottle of wine.

'You do have glasses don't you darling? And a bottle opener?' He turns towards me and poses prettily with his corkscrew held out towards me, obviously making sure Noah gets to see his best side.

'You know we do Freddy,' I respond a bit irritably, walking back over to the filing cabinet, which is also home to fifty dusty champagne glasses. 'You bought them for Kit's grand opening.'

'So I did,' he murmurs, sticking the unneeded bottle opener a bit hazardously in his pocket.

'Would you like a glass of wine Noah?' I ask, fully expecting him to make an excuse to leave. To my surprise he actually acquiesces and, taken aback, I glance round to see if he's simply being polite. After all, I'm sure he can think of better ways to spend his Sunday afternoon than in a scruffy office with three virtual strangers.

However, he seems perfectly at ease and his expression is one I've seen on him before and can only describe as interested enjoyment. With sudden insight, I realise that he's not looking down at us, rather he's actually taking great pleasure in meeting new and different people - completely out of the limelight.

Tucking two glasses under my arm and grabbing another two, I kick the cupboard door shut and take them back to the table where Freddy is now busy opening the bottle with a flourish.

'God, you're such a diva,' I hiss as he pops the cork as though it's a bottle of twenty five year old Châteauneuf-du-Pape (was that a good year…?)

'Why are you dressed like a bag lady?' he hisses back. I open my mouth to deliver a stinging retort, then glance down at my old faded cardigan. 'What's wrong with my clothes?' I ask finally in an indignant undertone. 'Beige cardy, baggy jeans and trainers. Do I need to say more?' And with that, he takes two of the glasses and turns his back. 'Bitch,' I mumble, picking up the remaining two…

The next couple of hours are actually great fun. Freddy is on top form, playing to the crowd – even if it is only an audience of three - and Noah seems more than happy to join in the banter, even taking some good natured ribbing about his sex symbol status. I'm perched up on my computer table and as I watch the teasing, I can't help but reflect just how surreal this all is, especially listening to Noah poking fun at himself. The overwhelming impression he gives is that, he might well be a famous movie star, but at the end of the day he's just so *normal…*

Luckily the gallery remains quiet and at five pm Kit goes through into the shop to close up. To my consternation, Noah gets up to follow her through and I'm not sure whether I should tag along too. I jump off the computer table, and feeling the now familiar, not to mention patently ludicrous, stab of jealousy, I hover at the office door uncertainly and watch as Noah wanders around the exquisite sculptures and works of art on display while Kit closes and locks the front door. After throwing the final bolt, she walks over to join him as he finally halts in front of the china clock that caused so much stress earlier.

After studying it for half a minute, he glances down at Kit and says drily, 'I think it might be a good idea, especially for your nerves, if I took this clock off your hands?' Kit stares up at him, her eyes shining and her mouth in a delighted smile. My heart lurches as he grins back. Feeling suddenly cold and a bit sick, I huddle into my cardigan and turn away from the door, only to pause as his voice calls my name.

'What do you think Tory? You're head of my design team of one. You think this will look good in my house?'

My heart lurches again, this time for a completely different reason and I all but skip over to them in my eagerness. If I had a tail, I'd be wagging it. Taking a step back, I hear Freddy walk up behind me as I pretend to study the clock from a slight distance. 'If I throw you a ball, will you run after it?' he murmurs from just behind my right ear. I resist the urge to step back again, this time directly on his foot, and opt for completely ignoring his bitchy comment.

'Yeah, I think it would. Maybe in the hallway. It's quirky, just like the spiral staircase.' And, actually, I really do mean it. Kit turns and gives me a warm grateful look and I feel like some kind of bunny boiler. God I'm a shit friend.

'That's it then, sold. Do you think you could box it up and store it here until Tory's ready for it?' I try for serious at his insinuation that I'm in charge as I look over to wait for Kit's answer, but fail miserably, and in the end we just stand grinning at each other. 'No problem,' Kit manages at length and turns back towards Noah. 'Thank you so much for your business sir, it really is very much appreciated.' Noah smiles and waves away her effusive thanks. 'Do you take American Express?'

Twenty minutes later, I reluctantly start making a move to go as I promised dad I'd be back for a cosy dinner with him and Mabel. Luckily they're going to the pics after so the torture is not going to be too prolonged.

To my delight, Noah offers to walk with me, citing the need for one last look over his lines before filming starts tomorrow.

'What time do you kick off in the morning?' I ask putting Dotty's leash on.

'Make up starts at four thirty,' he answers and all three of us shudder in unison.

'Well don't make too much noise,' I say in mock seriousness, 'I've no intention of climbing out of my nice warm bed until at least half past eight.'

'Mmm, think maybe I should crack the whip now you're working for me and come and give you a shake at six.' I resist the urge to nod enthusiastically at the thought of any shaking and whipping involving Noah Westbrook and my bedroom, and simply laugh. Unfortunately Freddy has no compunction about dropping me right in it.

'Of course you could always stay over,' he says cheekily. 'Then you could wake each other up…'

I glare at my so called friend, promising dire consequences to come if he doesn't shut his gob. Now. I daren't even look at Noah.

Grabbing Dotty's leash, I give Freddy one last scowl and head to the door for Kit to let us out. Once outside, I risk a glance at Noah and notice he's replaced the silly hat. He doesn't look pissed off. In fact he looks deep in thought.

'Thanks for coming for tea this afternoon.' I mumble, more to break the silence than anything.

He looks over at me and smiles. 'Thanks for inviting me. I've had a great time.' He sounds like he really means it. I smile back and we walk down towards the water front in companionable silence. The wind has died and the sun is trying to peek through the low grey cloud causing streams of sunlight to shine down on the water. Once at the river, we have to part company. We stand in slightly awkward silence for a couple of seconds, then he bends down and fusses Dotty. As he straightens, to my immense surprise, he kisses my cheek. 'See you tomorrow Tory,' he murmurs. I nod my head mutely for a couple of seconds until I realise that I probably look like one of those nodding dogs and manage, 'Yeah, have a nice evening Noah.'

Then I turn away before I fling my arms around his neck and beg him to take me home with him.

Desperation is so unattractive...

Half an hour later I'm doing my usual wheezing act up the garden path (really can't understand why I don't lose weight). The patio area next to the house is still buzzing with people, lights and equipment. As predicted, Noah's trailer is taking up the whole of the drive to the right of the house. It's absolutely massive and I have nothing but admiration to the driver who managed to get it in without actually knocking one of the walls down. I let Dotty off the leash, and she wastes no time dashing over to make friends with the crew who appear to be mostly standing around. As always, she's an instant hit and, leaving her to it for a couple of minutes, I go over and peek in one of the trailer windows. It's difficult to see much, but two things definitely stand out. Firstly, no expense has been spared, and secondly, cream leather appears to be the dominant theme. A completely different world.

Shaking my head ruefully, I turn back towards the house in time to see Dotty rolling around on her back in delighted abandon, being fussed by half a dozen people. She really is such a tart. Laughing I go over to introduce myself. Jed and Arnold are nowhere to be seen and I wonder if they're inside.

In fact, the inside is much, much worse than outside. The hall looks like a war zone. There are wires everywhere and Jed and Arnold seem to be in the thick of it. Giving them both a quick wave, I retreat hurriedly into the kitchen which is blessedly quiet compared to the rest of the house, and, apart from a large pile of used mugs, appears to have escaped relatively unscathed. I head over to the fridge to start preparing dinner, wondering what on earth dad was thinking, inviting Mabel over to this madhouse. I'm guessing, knowing my father, he thought she'd be impressed (that's if he did any thinking at all – not usually his strong point). Just hope she hasn't got a cleaning fetish...

I check my watch and note it's not yet six, still a bit too early to stick the pizza in the oven. (When I said preparing dinner, I meant in the very loosest sense of the word...) I wonder where dad is – I know he's not in the house, because there's no sign of Pickles, and believe me, Dotty would know if her hero was anywhere in the building.

Think of the devil... all of a sudden there's the sound of a banging door and my father's thundering voice.

'What a bollocking mess.' Then, as he crashes into the kitchen, 'I can't bloody well bring Mabel into this shit pit.' For once we are in complete agreement, although I probably wouldn't have phrased it quite so quaintly.

'Why don't you take her out for dinner?' I suggest calmly. 'I'll look after Pickles this evening while you and Mabel have a nice romantic meal followed by the cinema. How does that sound?'

He eyes me with a slight frown. 'Bloody suspicious.'

I sigh loudly and roll my eyes. 'Just what do you think I'm going to get up to?'

'Well it would be a damn change if you occasionally got up to something.'

'Ha ha,' I respond sarcastically. 'I think you get to misbehave often enough for both of us daddy dearest. And speaking of misbehaving – how are you feeling today? Slight headache perchance?'

'Never felt better,' is his infuriating answer. 'Anyway 'nuff about me. You heard from the actor?' His abrupt change of subject throws me for a second and I cast a mistrustful glance up at him. 'Why do you want to know? What's with all this sudden interest in my social life? I've told you exactly how things are between Noah and me. That's not going to change. You know it and I know it.'

'However much I might want it to,' I resist the temptation to add.

'What about these drawings he's asked you to do? What's that all about?' He's seated himself at the kitchen table and I can tell he's not going anywhere without some kind of explanation.

Sighing again, I put the kettle on. When my father's in interrogation mode, he's like a ferret and there really is no putting him off.

'He's thinking of possibly buying the house he's renting.' I hold up my hand as he opens his mouth to butt in. 'I said he's *thinking* about it.' There's no way I'm going to tell my father that it's all done and dusted. He could never keep that little gem to himself. Ever. But I can drip feed information to him, a bit like a carrot to a donkey. He'll keep quiet as long as he thinks there's bigger and better gossip to come. And of course, the threat of possible violence if he doesn't keep shtum, will no doubt help too...

'Bottom line is he's asked me to come up with a few ideas for possible improvements – to see if it's worth his time and effort.'

Handing him a cup of tea, I wait for the barrage of questions. To my surprise, he's actually silent for a moment which is so out of character I'm tempted to ask who he is and what he's done with my father...

Finally he looks up with a suspiciously deadpan expression. 'So that means he could be living here? In Dartmouth? Permanently?'

'I doubt it,' I respond, wondering exactly what's going on in that brain of his. 'I think he's just looking at it as a holiday home, or a bolt hole. Something like that anyway.'

He nods his head slowly at my answer but remains sitting with a pensive look on his face. My heart drops in response. That look never, ever bodes well. 'So, you pair are going to be thick as thieves while he's buggering about here then?' I sigh with exasperation. 'I've told you dad, it's not like that. He's asked me to do a job for him and I intend to do it. But – and please listen to this, because it's the last time I'm going to say it - That. Is. It...

'Now, are you going to take Mabel out or not? If you are, you need to get on the phone pronto.'

That does the trick. He looks at his watch and swears before clambering up and exiting the kitchen in pretty much the same way as he entered it. As the door slams, I hear him yelling, 'Who said you could turn my bloody study into a bollocking wardrobe?' Pickles hasn't moved. I swear that dog can understand English...

Chapter Fourteen

The next morning I'm woken early by the sound of voices. Loud voices. Glancing at the clock, I let out a small groan. It's six thirty in the morning for pity's sake. I try pulling the covers over my head but unfortunately Dotty's heard the commotion and decides to add to it by barking for England at the bedroom door. Unsure as to whether the din is going to completely scupper any filming going on, I leap out of bed and grab her. This wasn't something I'd bargained for, although knowing my dog's penchant for vocalizing every tiny bit of excitement, I really should have done.

I take her with me into the bathroom and turn on the shower. Hopefully the water will drown out both the commotion in the hall and Dotty's response to it. Good plan.

Ten minutes later I've thrown on my usual work clothes of shirt and jeans and, after opening the bedroom door a crack, I take a peek onto the upstairs hallway. With a sigh of relief, I note that there are plenty of people around but there doesn't appear to be any actual filming going on. With more confidence I open the door fully and carry Dotty out on to the landing. Once there, I take advantage of being unnoticed and, sitting on the top step with Dotty on my knee, I look through the banisters at the mayhem in the hall below.

There are several actors milling about dressed in early nineteenth century costume but I'm unable to recognize any of them from Saturday's cocktail party. Then, leaning further round, I spot Noah. He's dressed in classic Regency attire of a double breasted dress coat cutaway at the front and tails at the back over the top of a cream coloured waistcoat cut flat across the bottom. A white linen shirt with a simply tied white cravat complete his upper ensemble while close fitting pants and hessian boots the bottom. His hair has been cropped slightly and is now swept back in a cultivated tousled fashion, complete with discreet sideburns.

I stare at him fascinated. He is the epitome of a Regency Buck and my heart does a quick back flip as I watch him submitting with good grace to one of the make-up artists as she tries unsuccessfully to stop his unruly hair from falling into his eyes.

I'm not the only one eyeing the scene below however, and, as Dotty spots Noah, she jumps from my lap before I can stop her and dashes down the stairs. By the time I've reached the bottom of the staircase, she is happily ensconced in Noah's arms and is licking his face furiously, much to the chagrin of the two make-up artists still hovering around him. Laughing, Noah holds her away from his perfectly cut tail coat and hands her back to me as I rush up mumbling 'I'm so sorry , so, so, *so* sorry.'

Noah just shakes his head and grins at me, saying cheerfully, 'Don't worry Tory, it's only taken them two hours to get me looking like this.' As always my heart flips at his use of my name, and I smile back at him, uncertain whether he's joking or not. One look at the make-up artist's face however, has me beating a hasty retreat to the kitchen, promising faithfully to keep her on a leash next time.

Or maybe I should just move in with Kit while they're here. I think about it as I let Dotty out to do her morning business, and put the kettle on. I know my best friend wouldn't have a problem with me staying over, but it would mean not seeing Noah and I suddenly realize that I really couldn't bear that. Taking a deep breath, I finally acknowledge that I could well be in love with Noah Westbrook.

My heart sinks at this sudden epiphany. This really is not good, not good at all. 'No, it's not love,' I tell myself sternly, 'It's just lust, pure and simple. Lust...' And I slam the teapot down on the table as I repeat the last word out loud.

'Well, there's a word for seven o'clock in the morning.' I turn round in disbelief to see Noah leaning casually against the kitchen door. Damn. How the hell hadn't I heard him come in? Where's Dotty when I need her?

My face flames uncontrollably as I struggle to come up with some kind of explanation for my outburst. But, come on, who the hell can come up with an instantaneous reason for shouting out 'lust' to an empty room...?

Not me that's for sure. 'Do you want some tea?' is all I manage to finally stammer.

'Thought you'd never ask,' he responds with a smile, walking round the table towards me. Could be he hears the word lust regularly...

'I love your costume,' I say sincerely, letting Dotty back in, completely relieved to change the subject. 'You look like Mr. Darcy.'

'Wash your mouth out with soap,' he says with a wink, grabbing a biscuit off the worktop. 'Pride and Prejudice has got nothing on The Bridegroom. Are these ginger nuts?'

'Digestives,' I correct, 'And totally guaranteed to get crumbs all over your splendid tailcoat.'

'Give me the tea then woman, I'll just have to dunk.'

I hand him a mug. 'Careful,' I admonish lightly, 'Takes a much lighter flick of the wrist to dip a digestive successfully.'

Taking the mug from me, he deftly dunks the biscuit in and out of the tea and pops it into his mouth. I watch him with my mouth slightly open, totally spellbound.

Definitely lust...

'Practice makes perfect,' he grins, helping himself to another one.

'Are you allowed to eat anything while you're dressed up like a dog's dinner?' I ask, genuinely interested. 'Mmm,' he affirms round a mouthful of biscuit, 'as long as I keep the costume clean. Of course, if I spill something down it, I am assured of a long and horribly painful death. Why? Are you offering to cook me lunch?'

'Absolutely not,' I respond with a laugh. 'I'm sure you'll be partaking of a veritable banquet in that swanky trailer of yours. And anyway, I'm off to sort out your decorating.'

Noah opens his mouth to respond but is interrupted as a technician pops his head around the door. 'Mr. Westbrook, we're ready for you now,' he says with a slight apology in his voice.

'I'll be right there.' Noah answers the technician without turning. 'No rest for the wicked,' he sighs, quickly swallowing the rest of the tea and giving his last piece of biscuit to the furry dustbin at his feet. Then, giving me a small bow, he hands me the empty mug. 'Thank you sweet lady for the delightful beverage. And now I must bid you adieu as I go to earn an honest crust.'

I laugh as I watch him go.

I was wrong. Unfortunately, I really think it might be love...

~*~

It's five thirty pm and I've had enough. I've spent most of the day tying up all the loose ends of my other projects and have managed to arrange to meet with the architect and builder outside Noah's house tomorrow. I glance out of the small window at the back. The weather has been warm and sunny, in complete contrast to yesterday, and I really hope it continues tomorrow as we tramp around Noah's back garden.

All in all it's been a successful day – despite the efforts of my two best friends. Freddy must have popped in at least ten times on the off chance that Noah might be here, and Kit simply spent the whole day sighing and giggling.

Grabbing my bag and putting Dotty's leash on, I walk out into the gallery where Kit is just closing up. She and Freddy are heading straight to the Cherub to inform the pub's suitably impressed regulars that they now include Noah Westbrook in their circle of friends.

I said I'd pass...

As I walk onto the Higher Ferry, I hope against hope that Noah is still at the house. I have no idea what time they intend to finish filming today, but as long as I keep Dotty quiet and creep up the very edge of the garden, I reckon I won't be interrupting anything. From there, I can sneak into the kitchen.

Of course I'm telling myself that the reason I want to see Noah is to update him about my progress – yeah right...

The garden is deserted, all bar a lone camera man fiddling about with the lights as well as a couple of extras (well I haven't seen them before anyway) sneaking a crafty cigarette by the side of Noah's trailer, which seems empty, although the lights are on. After warning Dotty to be quiet, I let myself into the kitchen, only to come face to face with what appears to be the whole cast, being royally entertained by my father. Shit...

'Here she is,' booms my father in his best Admiral Shackleford voice (oh God, he's playing to the crowd, double shit...) 'The light of my life. My most treasured possession.' (Has he been drinking?)

Determined to nip my father's eulogizing right in the bud, I put Dotty down and ask only half jokingly, 'Haven't you lot got a movie to make?'

Turns out they're waiting for the light to change outside. Seems as if this whole filming lark involves an awful lot of waiting about. I look around for Noah and finally spot him leaning against a cupboard in the corner with his hand over one ear, obviously trying to have a conversation on his phone.

He is now dressed in the Regency gentleman's equivalent of evening attire and I can't help but stare. The whole ensemble fits him like a glove, right down to the skin-tight pants that leave absolutely nothing to the imagination. I swallow and wonder if I'm the only woman here who's suddenly finding it slightly difficult to breathe...

I glance back towards my father and note with relief that I'm no longer the centre of attention. Abandoning my defensive position at the door, I make my way towards Noah, intending to apprise him of today's progress. Six feet away I stop and hover self consciously, waiting for him to finish on the phone. Silently berating myself for not remaining by the door until he finished, I occupy myself by bending down to pick up Dotty. Not one for large crowds, she's been plastered to my side ever since we came into the kitchen – even the sight of Noah fails to elicit so much as the tiniest bark. Burying my head in her soft fur, I wonder where Pickles is. He's definitely not one for large crowds either.

Luckily, before I resort to dusting the dresser, Noah finishes his call and, turning towards me, offers a tired smile. 'Long day?' I ask sympathetically. He nods in response and steps closer to give Dotty a quick fuss. 'And it's not over yet. We're gonna be filming for most of the night I think. Hope your bedroom's not on the back.' I grimace in answer. 'Yep, directly over the patio. Still, I can always go stop over at Kit's.' I shrug my shoulders to indicate it's not a problem, then, looking round at the crowd loitering around the kitchen, I change the subject. 'How are you all going to eat?'

'The hotel's providing a buffet supper.' He glances down at his watch. 'Should be about sevenish.' I breathe a sigh of relief. My culinary skills would definitely not stretch to catering for this many people and besides, unless Dad's been shopping (and there's more chance of him going bungee jumping), we've only got a couple of pizzas in the fridge. I wonder if I can snatch a couple of picky bits from their buffet. Don't think I can actually get to the oven anyway.

Noah interrupts my musing, 'So, what progress have you made today. I'm completely prepared to be stunned.'

'Not sure I'd use the word stunned exactly,' I reply with a small smile, 'Maybe dumbfounded or perhaps flabbergasted are a little more accurate.' He raises his eyebrows and I laugh. 'Okay, let's settle on pleased. The fact is I've managed to arrange for an architect and builder to take a look tomorrow afternoon. Do you mind giving me a key?'

'Consider me officially impressed,' he answers. 'Quick work indeed. But are they any good?'

'I'd say so. I've used both of them before. I'll email you a couple of photos showing a couple of their completed projects and you can check them out on my website. So, will you let me have a key?'

He gives a mock sigh as I raise my eyebrows. 'Be gentle. This is a big moment for me. I've never given a woman a key to my house before.'

'What about your heart?' I quip back, then want to cut out my tongue.

'So, what are you two love birds having a little *tête*-à-*tête* about in the corner then?'

Heart in my trainers, I turn towards my thick skinned parent who is beaming at us both as though we've just got engaged. I can feel the anger start to swamp me, but I don't know who I'm more furious with – myself or my gob-shite father. I open my mouth to tear a strip off him, despite being in polite company; however, just as I get to, 'What the bl..' the kitchen door opens and in walks a blonde vision.

Gaynor Andrews is dressed in ice blue. The dress fits perfectly; low cut and gathered under the bust in traditional Regency fashion. Her hair is twisted up behind and falls down her back in a riot of soft curls and a bandeau of light blue twisted crepe and roses completes the ensemble. As one, the whole cast break into an impromptu applause.

Never have I hated anyone so much, or been so thoroughly ashamed of myself. I just have to get out of the room. Now.

I mumble something to Noah and back towards the kitchen table. All eyes are on Gaynor who is now holding court in the middle of the room, so it's relatively easy for me to scurry around the table and slip out of the kitchen behind her. I resist the urge to trample deliberately on her beautiful satin train as I push open the door, and loathe myself even more for wanting to...

Two minutes later I'm leaning against my bedroom door and take a deep breath. God I am such an idiot. I can see my shadowy reflection in the full length mirror on the opposite wall. The opposite of delicate. I look like a bloody farm hand. 'You silly cow.' I whisper to myself. 'You stupid, silly cow.'

I walk towards the mirror and continue out loud, 'So you're both best buds now are you? And what do you think's going to happen next then? He's going to fall in love with your "womanly curves"? Decide he prefers something to grab hold of in the sack?' I'm now right up against the mirror and want nothing more than to punch it. Then, incongruously I notice Dotty sitting shaking in the background, and just like that my anger dissipates, leaving a kind of sad acceptance in its wake.

Turning away from the mirror, I call the little dog to me and she runs up, tail wagging and rolls straight onto her back. 'Oh Dotspot,' I murmur, bending down to tickle her tummy, 'Your mummy's a complete and utter idiot. You'd think that at thirty two years old, she'd have more sense.' She licks my hand earnestly in answer. 'Well,' I continue standing back up, 'enough's enough. It's time to grow up. I'm not living in the middle of a bloody fairytale, no matter what Freddy thinks. Drop dead gorgeous world famous actors do not fall in love with nobodies – unless of course that nobody is someone with looks like Gaynor Andrews. And you know what Dot?' She looks at me with her head on one side as I wag my finger at her. 'My life is good. My life is happy. This job could put me on the map and I'm bloody lucky to have it. But that's all it is. A job. I'm not the first to experience unrequited love and I won't be the last. The sooner I get this sorted, the sooner he'll be gone and out of my life.' I nod my head at her emphatically. Excellent pep talk, don't you think?'

I completely ignore the little voice in my head that is saying, 'But what if he moves here permanently...?'

Chapter Fifteen

I wake up at six again, basically because I'm ravenously hungry. I didn't venture out of my bedroom again last night, so not only did I not get Noah's key but I didn't get anything to eat either, (not that it will do me any harm), and, once filming started I wasn't even allowed to turn on the bedroom light so I simply sat by the window in the twilight and listened to the dialogue taking place below. Of course it had to be a love scene. Talk about torture. Still, even self torment has its limits and after listening to the same protestations of undying adoration for the fifth time, I decided I needed to sleep…

As I get out of bed, I have the great idea of texting Noah and asking him to leave the key hidden outside his front door. That way I keep this professional and don't actually have to see him. Perfect plan. Maybe I should try starving myself more often.

Putting Dotty on her leash first, I peak over the banister. The hall below is deserted, and, breathing a sigh of relief I head down into the kitchen to grab something to eat. Contrary to my earlier speculation, starvation doesn't appear to be helping me in the thinking clearly stakes, as my stomach is now completely in charge and currently believes my throat's been cut…

I'm just finishing my tea and toast when the kitchen door opens, and, looking up with my heart in my mouth, I'm relieved to see it's Jed and Arnold. 'Hey,' I smile, 'How's it going guys. Want a cuppa?' At their nods, I set about making a fresh pot while they wax lyrically about Gaynor Andrews. Seems it's not only Jed's son who has a crush. After about five minutes of this,

I'm actually wondering if the person they're raving about is the same Gaynor Andrews who attended Noah's cocktail party. Maybe it's just overweight female interior designers she has an aversion to.

Another ten minutes goes by before I finally get them to draw breath long enough to ask what time they're kicking off today, only to learn that due to the late finish last night, and another one to come tonight, the intention is to allow Gaynor, delicate flower that she is, to get a bit of well earned beauty sleep and start just before lunch time. I nod sympathetically and resist the urge to stick my fingers down my throat along with an imitation gagging sound.

Think maybe I'm really not a very nice person...

My phone suddenly pings and, glancing down, I see that it's a text message from Noah. 'Oh be still my beating heart,' I gripe internally as I open up the message.

'Key under right hand plant pot – no-one will ever think to look there :-) If it's not too much trouble, stick around house til I get back?' I frown before replying.

'Rn't u filming l8 again tonite?'

'Not me. Gaynor's gig. Be finished bout 5ish. C u l8r. Will order us dinner.' Well, I'll be blowed...

After spending the morning at the gallery, I go back to the house to freshen up (go figure) before going up to Noah's. Plus I've decided to take the car and drive up. For two reasons. First of all, I don't want to arrive all hot and sweaty again and second, I might want to make a quick exit once we've finished talking shop over our cosy takeaway...

The unseasonably warm weather is still holding out which I think bodes well for Gaynor being stuck at the house until the early hours. Don't know whether to be happy or sad over that. I suppose it depends on whether I'm required to listen to her...

I change into a floaty skirt in soft pastels together with a fitted pale pink top and matching flat pumps. I actually dug it out from the back of my wardrobe – think I bought it for a wedding or something a few years ago. Looking at myself in the mirror, I reflect that even Kit couldn't complain at my image of feminine curvaceousness (is that a word?) Okay, it might be a bit dated but I think it's quite flattering. Makes me look younger too – always a bonus. Not totally sure that it's ideal tramping around a garden attire, but my wellies are in the back of the car.

I haven't actually told my best friend about Noah's text, his offer of dinner, or any of it really. She knows I'm taking the builder and architect round the house but that's all. I've never kept things from her before, and this is the second secret in as many weeks, but I just can't face coming back and dissecting it all with her and Freddy again. They'll want to know every little detail and I know I'll only end up bursting into tears or something similar – I've been making an idiot of myself far too often lately. This is simply business and I certainly don't tell her about every business meeting I have. Of course if she finds out, she'll kill me...

As I pick Dotty up to put her in my Ford Fiesta, I glance up at the high fence and gates shielding the Admiralty from the road. Just like the one at the bottom of the garden, the main gates now rival the entrance to Fort Knox, complete with a movie set equivalent of a bouncer stationed outside. Obviously the idea is that only those connected to filming are allowed within these hallowed grounds - which clearly does not include the local riff raff. I wonder if such a precaution is really necessary, but as he lets me out, I'm surprised to see that there is still a small contingent of hardened groupies milling around. Gives me quite a thrill actually to see them surge towards the car in the hope that it's someone famous. Unfortunately, there's pretty much complete indifference once they realise it's me - mind you, a couple of them do give me a wave which is rather nice...

Fifteen minutes later, I've driven round to Kingswear and am making my way slowly up along the cliff road to Noah's house. I'm a little early on purpose. I want to get a feel for the place again without all the Hollywood types diluting the atmosphere. After parking the car a few yards down the road (already laboriously turned around ready for the aforementioned speedy getaway), I hunt for the door key and find it under the pot as promised.

It feels strange letting myself into Noah's house. Although there's not a lot of furniture or decoration, the interior already feels infused with the actor's presence and for a couple of self indulgent minutes I allow myself to imagine living here with him as I wander from room to room. Then heading into the kitchen, I notice a half full bottle of red wine and two empty wine glasses, one with lipstick around the rim, and my day dream comes to a screeching halt. Telling myself it's absolutely nothing to do with me doesn't erase the ridiculous pain in my chest, but picking the glasses up and putting them into the sink makes me feel slightly better because I can't see them – how silly is that? Forcing myself back into professional mode, I take out my notebook and place it on the worktop. Then I do what we English always do when we're at a bit of a loose end – I put the kettle on.

By four thirty pm and three cups of tea later, both builder and architect have gone and I'm shattered but elated. They loved my idea of a full length outside porch and Edwardian conservatory but made suggestions and tweaks that would give both the added wow factor. We also came up with ideas for a completely new kitchen; master bedroom suite; three en suite bathrooms; new windows; bi-fold doors to the drawing room; a gymnasium and a tennis court. And that's just for starters. Woo-hoo, I'm on a roll. God, I'm good...

Heading back into the kitchen after seeing both men out, I ponder whether to make another cup of tea but decide I'm awash with Tetleys. That leaves either chocolate or alcohol. Can't see any chocolate, so I make a beeline for the half opened bottle of wine left on the counter. I hesitate briefly as I grab a clean glass and pick up the bottle but then, oh sod it, I'm sure Mr. Westbrook can afford it. I fill the glass, take a healthy swig and sigh. Just what the doctor ordered.

I take my glass and the rest of the bottle into the drawing room where Dotty is snoring loudly on the sofa. She had a field day earlier while we were outside, exploring all the interesting nooks and crannies of Noah's garden and is now completely pooped. Smiling, I sit down beside her and take another sip of wine. Within half an hour, the bottle is empty and I'm feeling pleasantly mellow and only vaguely aware that I've now gone and scuppered any chance of a quick getaway – or any getaway at all involving my car... Still, I can't really remember why it was so important, or why I have the word "professional" dimly rattling round in my head. Glancing down at my watch, I note it's already five thirty and wonder where Noah is. I lean back and consider ordering a taxi but it all seems an awful lot of trouble and I'm just so tired after hardly sleeping at all last night. I decide to close my eyes, just for a few minutes...

In my dream I can hear Noah calling my name, and Dotty's excited barking. I've been waiting for him for what seems like forever and I'm so happy he's home...

...Still half in the throes of my dream, I stare dazedly into the pair of incredible blue eyes just above me and with a smile, I reach up and bury my hands in his soft shining mane of black hair, whispering, 'I've been waiting for you,' before pulling his head down and placing a soft welcoming kiss on his lips.

At the exquisite sensation of our mouths touching, I come fully awake and, with a small gasp, start to pull back.

Eyes now glittering with some unnamed emotion, he holds me still and then, all at once he's kissing me desperately and I'm completely lost in a magical world of lips and hands and hot muscled satin skin. Somehow, I end up naked under him on the floor and then it feels as though he's stroking, touching, kissing me everywhere at once, finding every sensitive spot, tormenting every nerve ending until every fibre of my body is alive with hot, electric sensation. Groaning, I rake my hands down his back, at the same time arching my aching breasts up to his waiting lips. My legs part and curve around his thighs in instinctive invitation and I feel his body, the entire deliciously naked length of him press hard against me until, at last, there is that glorious welcoming fullness taking me to heights I've up to now only imagined existed.

Afterwards, lying in his arms, I go over every moment and commit it to my heart. If this never happens again, I don't want to forget one single second. But when the cold begins to seep in, and I make a move to extract myself, he turns me towards him and whispers, 'Stay.'

~*~

I have time to register that the light is much brighter than usual before Dotty's tongue resumes its enthusiastic licking of my nose. Blinking, I push her off, wondering for a second where the hell I am, then I recall last night and I sink back against the pillows in Noah Westbrook's bed, my mind awhirl with ecstatic disbelief. Glancing to the empty space beside me, for a second my heart sinks until I see the note on the pillow.

Sorry Tory, early start. Dotty's done her business, make yourself at home. Hope you enjoyed last night as much as I did. Will call you when we finish filming for today. You fancy dinner? Maybe somewhere nice and discreet so I can ditch the disguise…xx

Well, shiver me timbers and call me woody, as my father so eloquently puts it…

I can't stop smiling as my mind goes over and over the incredible night I've just had. I don't delude myself that this is anything more than a brief dalliance for Noah and probably similar to many he's had before me. But as I hug his pillow to my face and resolve to savour every moment I spend with him, I can't help but wonder if he's opened himself up to many other women the way he did to me last night. Maybe I was just in the right place at the right time.

I now understand the shadow of sadness that crosses his face when he thinks no one is looking. To lose a parent and an unborn child within an hour of each other would rock even the most solid world.

We spent most of the evening snuggled up together underneath a blanket Noah had unearthed from somewhere. We didn't bother to get dressed. Noah gave me an old t-shirt of his to wear like some ridiculous movie cliché. I had my bare legs draped over his knees as he talked in a matter of fact voice which spoke volumes of the pain he was holding inside.

Although it took quite a lot of wine before he began to speak, I sensed that he was really desperate to unburden himself to someone. Hard to believe that the someone he chose was me... Evidently the only other person he talks to is his sister in California, which is understandable. The loss of their mother especially must have had an equally devastating impact on her and I imagine the fact that one event lead to the other has made things even more difficult.

'I knew she didn't want the baby,' he murmured, taking a large sip of red wine. 'Said it wasn't the right time for her, that she had too much going on in her life right now, she had her career to think of. Well, you know what? It wasn't the fucking right time for me either, but that's not a good enough fucking reason. I spent hours trying to change her mind; said we could make it work. I thought I'd got through to her but then I got a telephone call saying she'd changed her mind.

'I was on my way to the hospital for one last try. Mom said she'd help me bring up the kid. All Gaynor had to do was give birth. That's all, just give it life.' I stifled a small gasp as he spoke the actress's name but I wasn't really surprised. Still, I said nothing and let him continue.

'I dropped mom off a couple of blocks from her house. She wanted to come to the hospital with me but I persuaded her not to. The traffic was awful and she suggested I let her out just off the freeway to save time.' He paused with a sigh and threaded his hand through his hair before leaning forward to pour us both some more wine. He handed me my glass without looking up and I touched his arm in sympathy. If he felt the contact, he didn't react, just continued in that same expressionless tone.

'If mom had come with me to the hospital she'd still be alive.

I left her trying to cross a busy road. Ten minutes later she was dead - killed in a hit and run.

'And I still didn't get there in time to stop Gaynor from going ahead with the termination.'

He fell silent and I had no idea what to say. I felt so desperately sorry for him and wondered how he had avoided the tabloids getting hold of the story. I guess his reputation for being one of the most private stars in Hollywood had obviously held true, no doubt with the sympathetic help a lot of loyal friends conspiring together to prevent the story becoming public knowledge.

Of course, I comforted him in the only way I knew how, and it's funny, but not once did my big bottom or over large boobs bother me in the slightest.

After disappearing off to sulk at the rare experience of being ignored for more than half an hour, Dotty came back as soon as we started eating pizza, determinedly pushing her way under the blanket until we took it in turns to spoil her with tidbits – totally against every doggy advice book ever published.

Later, over coffee, we talked about anything and everything, but I didn't ask him about his father and he didn't question me about my mother. I think we both felt we'd had enough sadness for one evening. Finally, at the end of the most amazing night of my life, we tumbled into bed and made love again, and again, and again...

And now he wants to take me for dinner. When the hell did I fall down the rabbit hole...

Friday 16th May

TO: kim@kimberleyharris.com

How's it going sis? Sorry I haven't been in touch for a few days, things have been crazy since we started filming.

I just wanted you to know that I'm good. In fact I'm better than good. I finally got things sorted with Gaynor; she came round to the house the other night and we talked. Think I finally got through to her that we're not gonna get back together. It's not even about the baby anymore and I sense she finally gets it. I really did love her once, but that ship sailed months ago.

And (he takes a deep breath...) I think I might have met someone. You remember me mentioning Tory Shackleford? Well, truth is we've been getting pretty close over the last couple of weeks while she's been organizing to fix up my house and she really is something special. I know she's not a typical Hollywood twig, but she's got some great curves going and has the most amazing smile. I really feel as if I can talk to her about anything - you know, it's like she's actually interested in me. She's just so down to earth, and she makes me laugh. I know it's early days but I'm thinking of asking her to come over to California to meet you guys. What do you think – you Ben and the kids up for that?

Like always sis, keep it to yourself for the time being – you're my rock, you know that.

I'm gonna be in Dartmouth for another couple of weeks, then it's up to London – I'll keep you posted. Wish me luck :-)

Give the kids a big kiss from me.

Love you loads

Noah xxx

Chapter Sixteen

'Well Jimmy there's something going off make no mistake, and what's more, I can tell you for nothing that none of it's good. For the last three days our Victory's been walking around like she dropped a penny and found a couple of grand. Every time she sees the package she gets this ridiculous grin on her face.' The Admiral sighed and took a deep melancholy swallow of his pint. 'When did it go so wrong?' He mourned to his bewildered friend.

'When did what go wrong sir?' Jimmy questioned with a frown. 'I thought this was what you wanted – you know, Tory getting off with Noah Westbrook and living happily ever after. Wasn't that the plan?'

The Admiral was obviously so depressed that he didn't even correct Jimmy's use of the package's name. When had it all gone tits up? Exactly when had his daughter become a loose woman? He looked over at his friend's confused face and sighed. This was exactly why he Charles Shackleford had finished his career as an Admiral and Jimmy Noon as a Warrant Officer.

Leaning forward he placed a hand on Jimmy's shoulder and spoke slowly and clearly. 'The package has obviously sampled the goods Jimmy boy. There's no doubt in my mind that my daughter is a fallen woman. She'll never get him to marry her now. The best she's likely to get is a centre spread in the Sun newspaper with a lurid red headline titled "The day I banged Noah Westbrook."'

Staring at his former commanding officer, Jimmy thought

back to his wife's description of Charles Shackleford. All of a sudden, the term "dinosaur" didn't seem quite so far-fetched. The Admiral had obviously never watched an episode of Coronation Street.

Jimmy was truly at a bit of a loss. To disagree would be considered insubordination and anyway he couldn't remember the last time he'd even thought about questioning the Admiral's logic. He glanced around the empty pub, stalling for time.

'Weeellll,' he finally said, dragging out the word as long as possible. 'The thing is Sir, I mean perhaps you should, err what I'm thinking is, I mean...'

'For God sake, spit it out man,' the Admiral finally interrupted with an irritated wave of his hand.

Taking a deep breath, Jimmy prepared to do the unthinkable. 'The thing is Sir, perhaps you should just let them get on with it now?'

The Admiral stared at his friend for a few seconds as if he couldn't actually believe his ears. 'Don't be so bloody ridiculous,' he said at length. 'Let them get on with it? What my Victory knows about relationships can be written on the outside of a flea's tit. If I let them just "get on with it", I know exactly what they'll be getting on with, and it won't end up at the altar I can tell you.'

Jimmy sighed. 'So what are you going to do Sir?'

The Admiral frowned and picked up his pint. Taking another long mouthful, he narrowed his eyes as the beginnings of yet another plan began to tiptoe around the edges of his mind. Then, replacing his empty glass on the bar with a decisive thump, he turned back to his friend.

'I think our package is in dire need of a nudge in the right direction Jimmy lad, and I'm just the man to do it...'

Chapter Seventeen

The last couple of weeks have been the best two weeks of my entire life. I've been pinching myself daily to be certain I'm not in the middle of some fabulous dream.

Not only did Noah take me for dinner, but since then, we've spent every bit of free time together, and the more I get to know him, the deeper I'm falling. It's not just about his film star looks, or his gorgeous sexy body. I know it sounds clichéd, but I really do like Noah the man. He's kind and smart and I can totally understand why the whole world loves him.

Why *I* love him.

Of course I don't allow myself to think too much about what will happen when he leaves for London, I'm just determined to enjoy whatever time we have together.

Despite the fact that we've been discreet, it's pretty clear that the rest of the cast and crew are aware of what's going on, although no one has commented, not even Gaynor. There seems to be some kind of unspoken rule that whatever goes on during filming stays firmly behind closed doors. I can't help but wonder if this is the normal situation. Perhaps big movie stars regularly pick on someone insignificant to "play with" while they're on location. I don't care. If that's the case, I'm simply grateful that Noah chose me – although I still have no idea why.

Even my two best friends are slightly baffled I can tell; happy for me of course, but still a little mystified. Though they'd done their best to set me up in the first place, I don't think either of them actually expected Noah to take the bait. After all, it's not like I'm a drop dead gorgeous human rights lawyer, like the one who finally got George Clooney to the altar...

But, like I told them both, 'If I'm just somebody to fool around with, I don't really need to be DDG.' I can tell they're both worried for me. They think I'll fall apart when Noah's gone. They might be right, but it's a risk I'm willing to take.

And at the end of the day, I will make his house so beautiful he'll never forget me. It's enough – it has to be.

Anyway, enough maudlin philosophizing, today is Friday and it's the start of the music festival. The whole cast and crew have been given the night off to relax and enjoy it. Apparently they're ahead of schedule and have only got a couple of loose ends to tie up before they move on to London next Tuesday. Noah and some of the crew are going to meet up with me, Kit and Freddy tonight and we're going to party...

We've decided to kick off in the Royal Castle. It's five pm and, not unexpectedly, Kit and I are first here. For once I've left Dotty with dad (or more accurately, Pickles) and as I push my way back from the bar, I reflect that this would be her worst nightmare. Handing Kit a large Prosecco, we clink plastic cups – the pub's sensible choice of alcoholic container for evenings as crowded as tonight is likely to be. 'To a memorable night.'

Sipping my drink, I try hard not to keep looking round for Noah, but Kit's not fooled. 'He'll be here Tory, don't worry.' She smiles at me reassuringly and I smile back with equal determination. 'Doesn't matter if he doesn't turn up Kitty Kat, tonight we're going to have a great time. Let's have a look at the program. Who's on at the bandstand later?'

Turns out Joey The Lips are playing. They're an 8 piece funk band, guaranteed to get the whole town boogying. Brilliant. Kit and I put our heads together to plan the evening up to then.

Stay in the Castle til sevenish with Spandex Ballet. Then it's on to the Cherub and spot of acoustic guitar; Kendricks for a bite to eat along with Joseph Bon Jovi and then back to the park and the bandstand to dance away the rest of the night to Joey The Lips.

Perfect – especially as the object of my desires is even now making his way through the crowds towards me, suitably disguised in his glasses and woolly hat.

I wonder how it can get any better than this...

Until I spot Gaynor Andrews following close on his heels, the black wig completely failing to disguise the unmistakable long legged skinny jeaned elegance. Damn...

I plaster a smile to my face, feeling plain and dowdy in my previously considered up to the minute v-necked sweater. Noah doesn't appear to think I look frumpy however, and he bends down without hesitation to kiss me lightly on the lips.

'You ladies have drinks right?' He says before wading his way through to the bar, unfortunately leaving Ms Andrews standing next to us looking as though she has a bad smell under her nose. After making the introductions, I look anxiously around to see if any of the crew are heading our way and thankfully spot Freddy, nautically resplendent in perfectly co-ordinated red and navy, posing at the door. Never have I been so glad to see him and I wave frantically, causing him to raise his eyebrows before picking his way nonchalantly towards us.

His composure definitely slips a bit as I introduce Gaynor to him, but after a small excited, barely perceptible skip, he recovers his self control with admirable aplomb and sets out to charm the actress in the way only a gay male can. Leaving Kit and me breathing a sigh of relief.

Unobserved, I stare at Gaynor as I sip my drink. It's the first time we've been in the same room since Noah confided in me about their baby. Although he made it clear that there is no longer anything between them, the subject has not been brought up again since that night, and I can't help but wonder how it feels to have loved and lost someone like Noah Westbrook. Despite his assertion that their relationship is definitely over, I know in my heart that Gaynor has not yet given up and her presence here tonight is definitely making me anxious.

By the time Noah has pushed his way back from the bar, half a dozen cast and crew members have joined us and the pub is getting seriously crowded. Completely unnoticed by other revelers, we all wedge ourselves in a corner near to the live entertainment where a raven haired Tony Hadley look alike is busy getting himself set up along with the other two members of Spandex Ballet.

A few minutes later, anybody over the age of fifty unlucky enough to be within earshot of the enthusiastic tribute threesome is facing the real possibility of ending up in the local hospital with suspected heart attacks as the band unexpectedly launch into their first number, shouting 'Gold' at a level of at least a hundred decibels...

...And most of those who survive the initial onslaught appear to be liberally covered in each other's drinks.

'Bloody hell,' mouths Freddy over the noise, after extracting the remnants of his plastic beaker from his top set of teeth. Luckily, most of his drink went down his throat unhindered, obviously due to lots of additional practice. Gaynor however, hasn't come off so fortunately, and her fitted little Lycra number is now soaked in red wine.

'Good job it's black,' mimes David Bollinger who providentially appears to have missed the worst of the initial blast while outside smoking a crafty cigarette.

Gaynor is furious, I can tell. However, the ear pounding sound track precludes her from complaining out loud and she resigns herself to shoving her now empty beaker at David and stomping off in the direction of the door – presumably heading towards the ladies.

I look towards Noah, wondering what he thinks of Gaynor's petulance, only to find him grinning at David and holding out his own cup to the director with the clear insinuation that 'if you're going to the bar anyway...'

Sighing, David signals that he'll bring back a couple of bottles. He points to my beaker, and I mouth 'Prosecco' while pointing at myself and Kit. Giving me a thumbs up, he disappears back towards the bar.

Despite the lack of conversation, I'm really enjoying myself. Noah seems completely happy to stay by my side, even going as far as resting his arm casually over my shoulder to pull my body towards his. I can't help but think that his show of affection towards me is the best disguise he could possibly have – no one in their right mind would expect him to be out with a chubby local girl…

Makes me smile actually.

Gaynor comes back just when I begin hoping that she's decided to call it a night, and hard on her heels is David, precariously holding a tray with four bottles on it. He waves at everyone to help themselves, after first diplomatically replacing his leading lady's empty beaker with a generous measure of red wine. Handing it to her, he leans forward to whisper something in her ear. I have no idea what he's saying, but, whatever it is, she blushes prettily and seems to relax.

As the director glances back towards Noah and raises his eyebrows, I register that it's probably almost a full time job simply to keep Gaynor happy and content. I try very hard not to feel slightly superior to the volatile actress but, to my shame, I fail dismally and, shrugging my shoulders, decide to just enjoy it while it lasts, as it's unlikely to be very long…

Turning towards Kit, I shout in her ear and she frowns in response. I try again and she shakes her head, pointing towards her ear. Sighing I try once more.

'I SAID, I'VE GOT TO TAKE A WHIZZ,' I yell, just as the band finishes the final note and the whole pub goes completely silent.

Yep, superiority short lived indeed.

As Spandex Ballet finish their second set, we decide to move on to give our ear drums a well earned rest with some acoustic guitar. Unfortunately, The Cherub is absolutely rammed up to the door so we elect to stay outside and send a couple of the crew to run the gauntlet to the bar.

The early evening is still pleasantly warm and the soft plaintive guitar music coming from the dim interior of the old pub is just enough to provide an atmospheric background, enabling conversation to flow once more. Somehow Noah and I get separated and, as I glance around, looking for him, my heart wobbles slightly as I see him in deep conversation with Gaynor. Whatever it is they're saying is evidently pretty serious if Gaynor's expression is anything to go by. Surreptitiously I watch, feeling a bit like some kind of stalker. I'm unable to see Noah's face as he has his back to me but I hope with all my heart that he is not staring at her with the same intensity that she's gazing at him.

Then suddenly she smiles, putting her hand over his arm and squeezing. I close my eyes and look down. I feel like my heart is being compressed – slowly, in a vice...

Fortunately, before I get too dejected, our two intrepid alcohol couriers arrive back, each holding a tray full of drinks – not a drop lost between them. As they are forcibly regurgitated through the door and out of the pub's jam-packed interior, the daring duo are treated to spontaneous applause. When the clapping dies down, I glance back towards Noah who, to my intense relief, has now moved away from Gaynor. He laughingly helps himself to a drink from the tray before pushing his way back over to me. I smile up at him, but as I lean towards his shoulder, I can still smell her perfume lingering on his arm and my apprehension increases.

'Is everything okay with Gaynor?' I ask softly. As he looks down at me, I wonder briefly if I've overstepped the mark, but after a second, he answers with a sigh, 'Yeah, it's good.' However, he doesn't elaborate and I can't help but reflect on how little I really know about him.

Still, now is not the time for brooding and I smile and squeeze his arm, while shoving away the thought that I'm the second woman to do that in the last fifteen minutes...

With drinks finished and no one else willing to brave the mass of humanity still squashed inside, we decide to head over to Kendrick's and dinner. We've booked a private room upstairs – hopefully we'll still be able to appreciate Joseph Bon Jovi without potentially suffering permanent ear damage for the privilege.

As we walk down the narrow street towards the restaurant, Noah drops his bombshell. 'Hope you don't mind sweetheart, but I invited your dad and Mabel to join us for dinner.' I can't help it, I look up at him in horror, causing him to laugh out loud. 'Tory, you look like I've just asked Jack the Ripper to eat with us. I just wanted to buy your father dinner as a thank you for letting us use your beautiful house.'

'He's getting paid for it,' I mutter.

Noah simply laughs again and pulls me towards him. 'Don't be a sour puss,' he murmurs in my ear, 'You know how much I love your smile. And anyway, I think your old man is a blast – he's always the life and soul of the party.'

'Yeah, that's exactly what worries me.' I reluctantly yield a small smile – more like a grimace really. 'Believe me, you've only seen the tip of the iceberg when it comes to Admiral Shackleford in all his glory.'

He grins again, looking like a mischievous boy. 'That's what I'm banking on darlin'.'

I sigh, knowing when I'm beaten. I just hope that dad hasn't left Dotty and Pickles with free access to chewable camera and sound equipment...

We arrive at Kendrick's slightly earlier than our booking at seven thirty but the speed at which we're ushered upstairs makes me believe that our host, Antoine, knows more than he's letting on – still, I suppose it's not rocket science given the number of American accents in our party.

We've been given the whole of the restaurant's first floor and the creaky wooden floor, open fireplace and sloping ceilings in the medieval building are your average American's dream. A large table has been set in the centre and everyone seats themselves higgledy piggledy. Noah and I are sat in one corner with Kit next to me and Gaynor at right angles next to Noah. Freddy has maneuvered himself to the other side of his new screen idol. Every seat is occupied except for two over the other side of the table. I don't know whether to be relieved or concerned that my father and Mabel will be seated so far away from any kind of control. Still, they're not here yet – they might decide not to come. Maybe a short prayer is in order?

Ten minutes later, the waiter has taken our drinks order and I'm starting to relax. Dad hates being late for anything – must be the military in him – and it really is beginning to look as though they're not coming.

Unfortunately, my relief is short lived as I hear a sudden commotion downstairs.

'Bloody hell, it's a real cake and arse party out there.' The Admiral's strident tones are completely unmistakable, as is Mabel's accompanying titter.

'I'll have a bottle of your red and don't give me any of your froggy grog Antoine.' He pronounces it Antoyne. The whole of the upstairs starts to shake as my father stomps laboriously up the ancient spiral staircase to the first floor with his hands on Mabel's bottom. 'Come on old girl, not far now, let me give you a leg up...

'Apologies for being adrift ladies and gents,' he pants, finally reaching the top floor. 'Had to get Jimmy to row us over – you should see the bloody ferry queue on the other side. Hope you lot haven't ordered yet, I could eat a scabby donkey between two mattresses. And I don't want any o' that bunny grub either.'

I wince inwardly but say nothing, silently wishing that Jimmy would once in a while get a backbone where the Admiral's concerned.

'Anyway, we're here now and that's all that matters,' he continues, holding on to Mabel's arm who looks as though she might fall over if she doesn't sit down soon. Suddenly concerned that it could possibly be back down the spiral staircase, I stand quickly with the intention of helping her to her seat. However, for the first time I can remember, dad seems to be showing concern for someone other than himself and he tenderly assists his shaky partner to her chair, throwing out introductions as he does. There's a brief wobble as she actually attempts a small curtsy but luckily she finishes up with a thump on the seat.

I breathe a sigh of relief and sit back down. Frustrating though my father is, the last thing I want is for his girlfriend to keel over in public (or of course in private – I'm not completely insensitive). Luckily, the waiter arriving with our drinks and menus gives Mabel a much needed opportunity to get her wind back without the possible need for the kiss of life.

Joseph Bon Jovi begins his performance with a lively interpretation of Keep The Faith and everyone settles down to enjoy themselves.

A couple of hours later, we've been fed and watered and we're ready to boogie. My father has announced to all and sundry that he's full to the gunwales, which I think is a less than subtle hint that he's had enough. Mabel however, has rallied round enough to pronounce that her dance moves were once commented on by none other than Margo Fountain and she is ready to kick up her heels. She's in such good spirits that I don't have the heart to correct her pronunciation of England's most famous ballet dancer.

Joey The Lips are already under way as we arrive at the bandstand, belting out Dancing In The Street to everyone in a three mile radius. We push our way in to the thick of it where Noah adds dancing to the long list of things he's good at and fortunately I've had enough alcohol to convince myself I'm Dartmouth's answer to Madonna.

An hour and a half later, completely pooped, Kit and I decide to take a breather and grab a hot chocolate from one of the street vendors, leaving Noah, Freddy and the die-hard members of the crew still strutting their stuff to Night Fever. As I slowly sip my drink, I look around for dad and Mabel, finally spotting Mabel nodding on a bench under the warmth of a halogen heater. I wonder where dad's got to – I wouldn't put it past him to be off phoning Jimmy with orders to row the dinghy back over the river to fetch them.

Turning full circle I finally spot him under one of the trees talking to Gaynor. My heart drops a notch as I wonder what on earth they've got to talk about, but just as I'm tempted to wander over to find out, Gaynor leans forward to peck my father on the cheek before walking away and disappearing into the throng of dancers. I stand and watch as he remains where he is for a few seconds before nodding his head slightly and walking back over to rouse sleeping beauty.

'What were you talking to Gaynor Andrews about?' The suspicion in my voice seems well founded when he jumps visibly at my approach. 'Bloody hell Victory, you trying to give me a coronary?' he grumbles, helping Mabel to her feet.

'What were you and Gaynor talking about?' I repeat my question flatly, refusing to be fobbed off. He gives a well practiced long suffering sigh which usually means he's frantically trying to come up with a story that'll wash.

'She was just thanking me for letting them use the Admiralty. Said how much she loved the house – actually wanted to know if I'd consider selling.' I narrow my eyes at him, searching in the gloom for any telltale clues that he's lying. 'Honestly Victory,' he continues in his best aggrieved tone, 'that's the gospel truth. I mean, what else would we have to talk about?'

I have to admit, he sounds plausible and I'm prevented from delving any deeper (which is usually when he's most likely to crack) by the arrival of Noah, Freddy and Kit. 'You two are looking pretty serious,' Noah murmurs, leaning down to give me a quick peck on my cheek.

I look up at him and smile, deciding to let the matter go for now. Noah will be gone in a few short days. There will be plenty of time for parental interrogation in the days that follow.

'How are you and Mabel getting home dad?' I ask instead.

'Ah, well, we're err, sort of, what I mean is, I'm staying at Mabel's tonight,' he finishes in a rush, looking for all the world like a guilty teenager.

I stare for a second, trying very hard not to picture my father and Mabel getting down and dirty in Mabel's bedroom (or anywhere else for that matter). I finally elect to ignore that possibility all together and focus on how they actually intend to get to Mabel's small terrace in Kingswear. 'Are you both going over on the passenger ferry then? You do know the last one leaves in twenty minutes right?'

My father glances down at his watch before saying, 'Bloody

hell Mabel, we better get our skates on or we'll be swimming.' Then without waiting to see his beloved's response, he takes off towards the river front like he's training for the Royal Marine Commando course.

Muttering under my breath about selfish irresponsible fathers, I gather Mabel's things to walk with her to the passenger ferry. To my surprise, Noah takes Mabel's arm, clearly intending to accompany us.

'You don't have to come with me,' I say, shaking my head for emphasis. 'I'll find you. It'll only take me half an hour to make sure they're both on the ferry.'

Noah gives a slight shrug in response. 'I'm getting a bit too old to dance the night away anyway, and it's way past my bed time. I'll be happy to walk you... both,' he continues turning to Mabel with a slight bow, instigating one of her infuriating titters.

I turn to Kit and Freddy, giving them a quick group hug. 'I've had a fab night guys, don't get up to any mischief after I've gone.'

Kit grins, then pecks me on the cheek before turning to Noah to do the same. 'Will we see you again before you leave?' she asks him. 'You bet,' he answers with a smile. 'Anyway, I'm practically a local. And don't forget, you owe me a clock.' Then, after succumbing with good grace to a kiss on each cheek from Freddy, he steers Mabel in the same direction as my dad, leaving me to follow with her handbag.

As I walk after them, I think about his comment about being a local. Does that mean we might not be over when he leaves for London? I can't help it, I experience a surge of hope. All of a sudden, anything feels possible.

As we approach the passenger ferry slipway, Noah hands Mabel over to my father who has obviously spent the last fifteen minutes hovering on the pontoon anxiously. Serves him right. Still, at least he didn't go ahead and board without her.

As they totter off, Noah turns to me. 'You fancy a moonlight stroll up to my house for a nightcap?' At my enthusiastic nod, we sneak on to the ferry after them, taking care to stay outside so we won't be seen.

Fifteen minutes later, we arrive at Kingswear. We decide to hold back for a few minutes before disembarking to give my father and his paramour a head start. 'Watch yourself Mabel, it's like the bloody black hole of Calcutta up here,' are the last words we hear from the Admiral as they disappear. We glance at one another and exchange grins as we finally go ashore.

Crossing the road next to the lower car ferry, we walk hand in hand under the arch next to the small post office. The air is redolent with the scent of honeysuckle as we turn left to walk up the Alma steps following the lane which eventually turns into a private road winding around the cliffs towards the mouth estuary. The road is dotted with the most amazing houses, each one more stunning than the last, culminating at Noah's, just before the coastal path begins.

It's unbelievably romantic. The moon is almost full and the sky is totally clear and filled with stars. I don't think I've ever been so happy. Out here, I can forget that Noah's a famous movie star and just make believe that he's my partner and we're simply walking back home after a wonderful night together.

I sneak a glance up at his profile which suggests he's deep in thought. 'Penny for your thoughts,' I say softly, squeezing his hand lightly. He tightens his hand around mine in response as he smiles down at me, eyes almost indigo in the bright light of the moon.

'I was thinking about London,' he answers, turning back to look up the road. My heart drops as I presume he's already moving on from me. From us.

Which makes his next words all the more shocking...

'I was actually wondering if you'd like to come up to London to stay with me – maybe next weekend?' Unable to stop myself, I halt and stare up at him with my mouth open in amazement. Looking down at me, he actually laughs out loud. 'I really do love that look on you Tory,' he teases, 'sort of like a fish.' But this time I'm not really listening, my mind is playing the words 'Come and stay with me,' over and over.

'Well?' he asks finally, when I fail to respond. 'Well what?' I whisper back distractedly, still unable to get my head around his request. Frowning slightly at my failure to answer, he places his hands on my shoulders and turns me to face him, peering at me closely before repeating his question.

'Will you come up and stay with me in London for the weekend?'

I gaze back up at his beautiful, serious face, my mouth suddenly as dry as Ghandi's flip flop, and somehow manage to croak, 'Yes.'

Friday 30th May

To: kim@kimharris.com

Hey Kim

How's it going? It's three in the morning here and I can't remember the last time I was this happy. Maybe that's why I can't sleep :-)

Remember how it felt, the night before the holidays started, how we used to lay awake, too excited to sleep? That's how I feel.

I've just had the best night at this crazy music festival they got going here in Dartmouth. The only bug in the ointment was you guys not being with me, but next year, I'm flying you all over here. You'll love it Kimmy, and I know you'll love Tory. She's the one sis. I never thought I could feel like this.

I told Gaynor how I feel about Tory tonight and she was totally fine with it. I even admitted I'd told Tory about what happened with mom and the baby and she was good. Said it was great I found someone I trusted enough to open up to, and she knows that one day she'll find someone equally special to confide in.

I feel like a great weight has been lifted off my shoulders sis and I can't tell you how good that feels.

Will call you from London.

Love you all loads

Noah
xxx

Chapter Eighteen

'It's all set up Jimmy lad. Keep your eye on the news, there's going to be an interesting announcement very soon followed by the sound of wedding bells, you mark my words. All he needed was a nudge in the right direction'.

The Ship was pretty much empty despite it being Friday lunchtime, the whole of Dartmouth and Kingswear still getting over the music festival the weekend before. The barmaid had disappeared to make the two men a cheese and onion sandwich – a cunning ploy by the Admiral to get Jimmy on his own without anyone ear wigging.

Jimmy frowned at the Admiral's self satisfied tone, feeling a not unfamiliar sinking sensation in the pit of his stomach.

He knew that if he was to stand any chance of finding out just what his friend was up to, he'd have to play it cool. The Admiral wouldn't be able to resist boasting about his supposed ingenuity if Jimmy played his cards right, and this was a game the smaller man was well accustomed to.

Sure enough, Jimmy's disinterest prompted the expected glower, together with an irritated humph, and only the arrival of their doorstop sandwiches postponed the predicted blowing of the Admiral's trumpet.

Once the barmaid was out of earshot, the Admiral took a bite out of his sandwich and leaned towards Jimmy, tapping the side of his nose.

'I've given a small tip off to this journalist chappy,' he murmured, inadvertently spraying bits of bread and cheese liberally over Jimmy's sweater.

Jimmy puckered his brow, processing the Admiral's information while absently brushing the crumbs off his jumper. 'What journalist?' He asked finally, prompting an impatient grunt.

'Does it matter? The point is, Jimmy lad, this reporter was very interested to hear about a certain romance if you get my drift...'

Jimmy paused, sandwich in hand, and stared in horror at his former commanding officer. 'What the bloody hell's wrong with you?' The Admiral demanded when Jimmy returned his sandwich to its plate untasted.

Jimmy carefully wiped his hands on his paper napkin while his mind frantically tried to process the enormity of the Admiral's interference. Silently he tried to come up with some sort of excuse that would explain and justify his oldest friend's meddling.

In the end, all he could think of to say was, 'You shouldn't have done that Sir. You should have left well alone. Tory's a sensible girl, and she's perfectly capable of running her own life without your interference.' Then he climbed down from his stool, bent down to give Pickles a quick head rub, before straightening up and staring his old commanding officer in the eye. 'You've been like a brother to me Sir, for more years than I can remember, but I'm very sorry, on this occasion, I can't condone your actions Admiral. Permission to withdraw...'

The Admiral stared aghast at his friend. This was insubordination at its absolute worst. He had no idea what to say.

In the end, it wasn't up to him. Jimmy saluted smartly, and walked away.

Chapter Nineteen

It's seven thirty in the morning and I'm lying in bed listening to the unaccustomed silence. Noah's finally gone to London. In the end we had a whole extra week together thanks to a few more loose ends than anticipated, but now the whole cast and crew have relocated to Greenwich in London. The only reminders of the last few weeks are a few trailer tire tracks, and the newly erected six foot gates that are likely to last longer than the house.

I couldn't be happier.

For some obscure and totally crazy reason, Noah Westbrook likes me. I mean, *really* likes me. ME – plain, plump, ordinary Victory Shackleford. Since leaving for London, he's phoned me at least once a day, sometimes as many as four or five times in between filming. And this weekend I'm going to see him again. He's rented a mews house in South Kensington where we can be completely alone and away from prying eyes. I feel as though I'm living in some kind of fabulous dream and keep thinking any moment now, I'll wake up and find out it's all been in my head.

Today is Monday so I've got four whole days until I see him again. Lots to do until then if I want to show him some progress on the house. Jumping up, I oust a still snoring Dottie from the cocoon she's made of the bedclothes, and head to the bathroom singing.

Fifteen minutes later I'm grabbing a piece of toast en route to an early start at the gallery. There's no sign of dad which is a little surprising. He's usually ensconced in the kitchen reading his newspaper by now. Taking a bite of toast, I frown a little, wondering if he's gone out early with Pickles, then I shrug – trying to second guess my father is like trying to slam a revolving door. Leaving him a quick note, I put Dotty's leash on and slip out of the back door into the garden.

It takes me twenty minutes to reach the other side of the river, and, once on dry land, I stop in the local French deli to buy a couple of pain au chocolates, still deliciously warm from the oven at this time in the morning. There are a few people waiting as I enter the shop, and to my surprise they stop chatting, and turn to stare at me as I walk in. I glance down to check I haven't left my skirt tucked into my knickers – wouldn't be the first time - but all appears to be where it should be. As I join the queue, the silence starts to become slightly oppressive, and I have no idea what's causing it. I step forward to place my order with the lady behind the counter. As she hands me the warm bags, I attempt a smile to lighten the atmosphere, and I'm completely taken aback as she responds by giving me a broad grin and a wink. Smile faltering, I back out of the shop, juggling my packages as I fumble to untie Dotty from the lamp post. Hurrying away, I hear one of the customers say in low tones, 'Bloody unbelievable.'

I walk quickly round the corner towards the gallery, anxious to get out of sight of eyes I can still sense staring at my back. The whole incident leaves me slightly unsettled, and as I go to unlock the gallery door, I'm surprised to find it's already open. Heart hammering at the thought that Kit could have had a break in, I cautiously shut the door behind me, and walk towards the back of the shop, all the while checking to see if anything is missing. As I push open the office door, I jump as a shadow rises from the chair.

'Bloody hell Kit, you nearly gave me a heart attack,' I gasp, 'I thought you'd been burgled.' I put my things onto the desk before continuing, 'You're in early, what's the occasion? Still, at least your pain au chocolate won't need nuking for a change. Have you put the coffee on?' Picking up the paper bags, I walk towards the kettle before registering that Kit hasn't answered.

Frowning, I turn towards my best friend to ask her what's wrong, but as I see her face, the words die in my throat. She looks so sad and my heart lurches as I read pity in her gaze. For me. Glancing down to the coffee table in front of her, I register the newspaper open at what appears to be a double page spread. I feel sick as my eyes travel back up to meet hers. 'I'm so sorry Tory,' she whispers, pushing the paper towards me. Dread mounting, I drop the bags and step forward until I'm standing over the open newspaper. The lurid headlines scream out at me...

NOAH WESTBROOK SET TO MARRY UNKNOWN BRIT IN DESPERATE BID TO PUT BEHIND HIM THE TRAGIC LOSS OF HIS UNBORN CHILD AND MOTHER ON THE SAME DAY.

Underneath is a picture of Noah entering a restaurant in London, together with a picture of me, taken God knows when, and a picture of a white faced Gaynor, hands up in an attempt to protect her from the camera.

I hear a low moan, and realise with a shock that it's coming from me. Grabbing the newspaper, I sink into the other chair.

The whole story is there, every explicit juicy detail. As I read the last few lines, I can feel the bile rising into my throat.

A source close to local girl Tory Shackleford says that the bride to be is understandably over the moon at being given this precious opportunity to help Noah get over the double tragedy, hinting at the possibility of more children in the not too distant future.

Both Noah Westbrook and Gaynor Andrews have declined to comment.

Flinging the newspaper away from me, I clutch my middle, and rock backwards and forwards, tears sliding unchecked down my face. I barely register Kit jumping up and going to lock the gallery door, before coming back to crouch in front of me, and pull my unresisting body into her arms.

'It wasn't me Kit, it wasn't,' is all I'm able to whisper, over and over again. Suddenly I pull away.

'Why hasn't he called me? He knows I wouldn't do this, he knows me. I have to phone him. I have to make him understand it wasn't me.' Ignoring Kit's advice to sit and think before I do anything I'll regret, I push her away and jump up to get my mobile phone. With shaking hands, I bring up Noah's telephone number. 'I'll explain it to him,' I mutter, pressing dial. 'He'll believe me, I know he will.' Taking deep panting breaths, I wait for the dialing tone. If I can just get to speak to Noah, everything will be okay.

'The number you have called has been disconnected.'

'No, please God, no,' I moan, trying the number again and again until Kit gently prizes the phone out of my hand, and puts it back in my bag.

'Stop, please stop Tory,' she begs, holding my hands between hers tightly. Leaning forward, she rests her forehead against mine. 'We'll sort it love, we'll do it together. You'll get through this, I promise.'

But I know she's lying. Nothing will ever be the same again.

~* ~

A couple of hours later we're holed up in Kit's flat. I think she called my father to tell him where I am. I didn't speak to him. I don't want to speak to anybody. The vultures are already descending on Dartmouth, looking for another scoop. I can't seem to think straight. My mind just keeps telling me I need to speak to Noah.

Kit has made several phone calls and tells me she's been unable to speak to the journalist who wrote the article. I can't even remember his name. I stroke Dotty's silky head absently as she presses herself up against me, sensing my distress.

'I have to go and see him Kit.' It all seems so clear suddenly. 'I have to go to London and speak with him.' I lean forward and clutch her hand, willing her to understand, to help me. 'I can't leave it like this. I have to make it right.'

I expect her to protest but all she does is sigh. 'Do you know where he is?' I nod eagerly. 'It's a small boutique hotel. Noah told me that David booked the whole place. Said it was tucked away, quiet, away from the cameras.' I laugh bitterly.

An hour later we're on the road. Kit insisted on coming with me, mostly I think because she doesn't trust me not to do something stupid. I didn't protest too much. The sick feeling in the pit of my stomach is telling me that the next twenty four hours are not going to be a high point in my life and while I may not be *that* stupid, I sense I'll need my best friend's support. We have left Dotty in the doting arms of Freddy, and I had to smile at her total absorption in the chicken sandwich he was eating as we left...

I sit silently while Kit is driving. I don't have any kind of plan, apart from somehow confronting him at the hotel. I have a feeling that I'll only get one chance, and I've no idea how I'll convince him of my innocence – or if he's even interested. I've googled the hotel, which is set on a discreet street in Belgravia. The website described it as timeless, a gentle ode to classicism, a place to relax and be waited on. Unfortunately, I don't think I'll be staying that long.

While driving in London is not for the faint hearted, and certainly not for people whose navigator is more interested in biting her nails down to quick than giving accurate directions, Kit is fortunately an old hand at negotiating Britain's capital city. Her eclectic travels in search of unique and distinctive pieces of art could potentially result in a successful career with Google Maps if the gallery ever closed down.

We finally arrive at our destination (or rather a back street half a mile away) in the middle of the afternoon. I have no idea of Noah's schedule, and I tell Kit that I'll simply find somewhere to sit where I can observe the hotel unnoticed until he turns up – in or out. I can see Kit's not happy, but one look at my face convinces her that arguing would be fruitless.

In the end, we find the Beckenham Hotel quite easily. Oozing quiet glamour, the Georgian townhouse is slightly set back from the road in a small leafy verdant garden giving the illusion that it's not in the city at all. As I stare up at the vintage exterior, I wonder which room is Noah's, and shiver. Then, looking round, I spy a small bench sheltering under a flowering hawthorn tree in the corner of the garden. While giving an unrestricted view of the quiet street, it's nevertheless almost invisible to anyone walking up to the hotel entrance. Gesturing my intention to Kit, I glance quickly back to the hotel entrance before slipping unobserved through the gate. The afternoon is cold and grey, which will hopefully put off anyone tempted to linger in the secluded arbour. After a few minutes hesitation, Kit follows me, and we sit huddled together to wait.

In the end, it's almost an anti-climax when I finally get to confront Noah after only a two hour wait. Despite it being early evening, the lane around the hotel is still deserted, only birdsong competing with the muted London tea time traffic a couple of streets away. I wonder where all the paparazzi are, and grimace when I realise they're probably all camped outside the Admiralty. There's no sign of any cast or crew either, and my nerves are stretching to breaking point. Then suddenly, without warning, Noah appears around the corner. Heart in my mouth, I watch him walk across the narrow road. He cuts a lonely figure as he strides towards the hotel entrance looking neither right nor left. I know he hasn't spotted me. Clutching my hands together, I step out of Kit's comforting presence, and stumble onto the path where he can see me easily. For a second, he doesn't register the movement, then he turns and looks straight at me. The remote, stone faced man standing ten feet away bears no resemblance at all to the warm, affectionate lover I knew in Dartmouth, and just like that, I know it's over.

I lurch forward, desperate to say something, anything, but as I move, he steps back. He stares at me coldly for a few more seconds before deliberately turning away, and walking up the steps to the doorway. Two minutes later, the hotel concierge appears at the entrance, and asks us politely but firmly to leave.

I don't remember walking back to the car, or negotiating the rush hour traffic to get out of the city. I just remember the shaking. At some point, Kit must have covered me in a blanket. I wanted to say thank you but I couldn't seem to muster the energy to do anything but huddle into it, and stare unseeingly out of the window. I think we finally arrived back in Dartmouth around midnight. I recall Kit giving me a small white tablet before putting me to bed in her flat, then only soft, welcoming blackness.

Chapter Twenty

I'm woken up by the bang and clatter of the weekly rubbish collection in the street below my window. Groaning, I turn over and pull the pillow around my ears. God I feel terrible, like I've just come off an all night bender. I briefly wonder why I'm lying in a strange bed, then it all comes crashing back, making me feel as though I've been punched in the stomach. Taking a deep breath, I roll onto my back and stare at the ceiling.

I don't know where to go from here. Being with Noah has changed me in ways I'm only now beginning to realize, and I don't have any idea how to pick up the pieces of my former life. It feels as though a door to an exotic wondrous dream has been slammed in my face. But at the end of the day, that's all it ever was – a dream.

A knock at the door puts an end to my self absorbed misery. I'm tempted to ignore it, pretend to be sleeping, but that's never kept Kit out before, so I sigh and reluctantly mumble, 'Come in.'

To my surprise however, my visitor isn't Kit, but Freddy. I look behind him but there's no sign of Dotty. 'Hope you haven't lost my dog,' I grumble, feeling suddenly naïve and foolish at the stupid, *stupid* situation I've found myself in.

'Dotty's out for a morning constitutional with her aunty Kit,' Freddy replies, perching on the side of the bed. 'You ladies may have risked life and limb pinning down a Hollywood super rat, but I've had a whole day of picking up dog poop. One day is enough.'

I close my eyes. Maybe Noah Westbrook is a rat, but in my

head I can still see him walk unsuspectingly towards my leafy hiding place, somehow looking so isolated and alone. Resolutely putting the picture out of my head, I make an effort at a smile, 'Thank you Freddy, your heroic sacrifice is duly noted, and a bottle of something nice will be heading your way as soon as I get out of bed.' I give an experimental tug on the bedclothes trapped under his bottom, but before I can tell him to shift, a white bundle of fur comes dashing through the open doorway, and with a flying leap Dotty throws herself at me, as though I've been away for weeks.

Her total joy at my mere presence brings a lump to my throat, and, swallowing the threatened tears, I grab hold of her wriggling body, and plant hello kisses on the top of her head.

Jumping up to protect his perfectly creased trousers from muddy paw prints, Freddy gives a dramatic, long suffering sigh before retreating to the door. 'I'll leave you two to get re-acquainted while I supervise Kit's regrettably lack lustre coffee making skills.'

An hour later, I'm showered and dressed in my less than fresh jeans and sweater from yesterday, sipping Freddy's unique interpretation of a caramel latte which, if my taste buds serve me correctly, includes a large slug of Grand Marnier. Sitting here with my two best friends arguing with each other over my best interests, I realize just how lucky I am. Whatever happens in my future, I know that Kit and Freddy will be there commiserating, celebrating, or cheering me on, and I'll be doing exactly the same for each of them. Who needs a man anyway...?

Unfortunately, the ringing of my mobile phone chooses this moment to reveal the utter sham of my burgeoning attempts at looking on the bright side, as my heart jumps in the hope that it's Noah calling to tell me it's all been a misunderstanding. I grab the phone without stopping to look at the caller ID and fight the urge to cry with disappointment as my father's deafening voice shouts down the phone.

'Victory is that you?'

Sighing, I hold the phone away from my ear before responding,

'Hi dad, yes it's me. Is everything okay at home?'

'Total cake and arse party over here girl. Whatever you do, don't come back. The bloody papa... parap... pazap... damn journalists are six deep outside the gates. Take a special ops exercise just to get you in. I'm sending Jimmy over with your stuff. Lie low, and I'll send a signal when it's safe for you to come back.' He puts the phone down before giving me any indication of what the signal is likely to be, and I'm left filled with apprehension at what exactly my father deems to be "my stuff"".

I look over at my two friends. 'I hope you're not expecting any guests over the next few days.'

~*~

By lunch time the next day, I'm ready to throw myself out of Kit's window. I haven't stepped foot outside since our return from London, and Kit has done everything in her power to keep me from reading any of the tabloids or watching the news. 'It's a nine day wonder Tory,' she answers airily when I protest. 'The bloody vultures will soon get fed up, and move on to torment some other poor sod.' I can only hope she's right, but that doesn't stop me from pacing the floor in her small flat and wondering, achingly, what Noah is up to right now.

That dad's interpretation of my stuff turned out to be surprisingly accurate hasn't helped the matter any. If my sixty five year old father is able to pack me a case, what does that say about my personality...? Drinking my umpteenth cup of coffee, I throw myself despondently into an armchair. The calls are stacking up. I've let most of them go to voice mail - including the builder and architect asking about Noah's house - but I can't hide forever.

Suddenly Dotty jumps up and starts barking as the flat buzzer rings, indicating a visitor. Kit is at the gallery, so I nervously pick up the receiver without speaking. 'Are you there Victory?' My father's total inability to do anything in a normal level of decibels causes Dotty to start a fresh round of barking. My heart sinks. I haven't seen him since all of this kicked off, and I know he's worried about me, but the thought of trying to make polite conversation with my dad fills me with complete horror.

'I've got a letter for you,' he continues, completely oblivious to my lack of enthusiasm. 'It's from London. Thought you might want to read it.'

Heart thumping, I immediately let him in. Maybe Noah's had second thoughts. While he's stomping up the stairs, I make a concerted effort to collect myself. It's probably nothing. As my father finally enters the flat, there's a moment of pandemonium as Pickles dashes round his legs to greet his long lost friend. Both dogs are ecstatic to see one another, and I close my eyes wearily as my father yells at them both to stop the bollocking noise – even though he's the one making most of it.

'Do you want a coffee?' I ask when the racket has died down slightly. I wander into the kitchen without waiting for an answer, and, hands inexplicably trembling, I put the kettle on. Dad follows me through and to my surprise, pulls me into a quick hug before handing me the envelope. Glancing up at his face, I notice how pale he is, with dark circles around his eyes. I narrow my eyes at him. 'Are you okay dad?' I ask, slightly worried. He waves my concern away however, and, pointing to the envelope, still unopened in my hand says abruptly, 'Open the bloody letter Victory and let's be done with this business.'

Frowning, I take a deep breath, and walking back into the living room, tear open the envelope. It has a London postmark. I quickly scan the contents, feeling completely sick.

The letter's not from Noah at all. It's from a firm of London solicitors asking me to cease harassing their client Mr Noah Westbrook with immediate effect. Should I fail to heed this advice, the matter will be reported to the police in relation to possible criminal proceedings. With regard to my employment by Mr Westbrook to project manage the renovations to his house in Dartmouth, I am advised that the house is being put up for sale, and my employment is now terminated. I will be allowed to keep the one hundred thousand pounds given to me at the start of the project as a good will gesture. However, should I attempt to contact or harass their client in any way, the funds will immediately become repayable.

Re-reading the letter, I sink into a chair. The bastard. He hasn't even given me chance to defend myself, he's just buying me off. Did I even know him at all? Allowing my head to sag against the back of the chair I give a small, bitter laugh, and throw the letter onto to the floor. 'Lucky me,' I whisper, 'I'm now a hundred grand richer. Not bad for a few shags, eh dad? Your daughter's going up in the world. You think I should open myself an escort agency, you know, specializing in larger women?'

My father stares at me for a second before bending down to pick up the discarded letter, and the room is blessedly silent for the next five minutes as he reads.

'What, nothing to say dad?' I ask sarcastically as he finishes reading. 'Bloody hell, that's got to be a first for you.' His face blanches slightly at my words but he stays silent, distress uncharacteristically written all over his face. I take a deep sigh, guilt gripping me. I know my father cares about me, and it's not like this situation is his fault. 'I'm sorry dad. I shouldn't be taking this out on you. To be honest, I'm angry at myself more than anything. I was just stupid to think we ever had any future, something like this was bound to happen.'

He opens his mouth to say something, but unable to face any more sympathy, I jump up to turn on the TV for the first time in days. 'Let's see what's going on in the rest of the world shall we? You watch while I get you that coffee' Then I flee back to the kitchen.

I can hear the daytime soaps in the background as I linger, dragging out the time it takes to add coffee and milk to the mugs, while waiting for the kettle to boil. Then, unable to make it last any longer, I take the drinks back in to the lounge.

As I hand my father his mug, he takes a sip, glances up at me, then coughs, clearing his throat. 'The thing is Victory,' he starts to say in a gruff voice, as I sit back down in my chair...

But whatever he wants to tell me is lost as the midday news

comes on. He begins to get up, obviously intending to turn it off, but I wave my hand at him. 'You can't all protect me forever dad. I need to know what's happening.' Frowning, he sits back down, but I can tell he's ill at ease. We sit in tense silence as each story comes up, but we have to wait twenty minutes for the interesting bit - I'm glad the world economy takes precedence over Hollywood gossip. Then my stomach churns as Noah's picture comes up on the screen.

'There have been no further developments in the Noah Westbrook story. The actor is staying firmly silent, as is his co-star Gaynor Andrews, although the two have been seen together on several occasions recently, sparking rumours that the stars intend to put their tragic past behind them and re-kindle their romance.'

A blurred photograph of me comes up on the screen as the commentator continues, *'Tory Shackleford, the other woman in what appears to be turning into a bizarre love triangle, has not been seen since the story broke, despite the continued presence of reporters outside the Dartmouth resident's house.'* The picture of me is replaced by one of the Admiralty, a dozen reporters still camped outside our bright shiny new gates.

'Bloody nightmare just to get out of the place,' my father grumbles, obviously uncomfortable. I don't know what to say. I daren't look at him. If I see any sympathy in his eyes, I know I'll break down. Instead I sit staring at the TV screen, where the news has now gone on to show a heartwarming story about a dog. A nine day wonder Kit said. She was right. And Noah and Gaynor are probably going to get back together. How funny is that?

'Fact is you're better off without him Victory,' my father blurts angrily when I fail to respond. 'These pretty Hollywood types aren't for you my girl. No idea about real life or what it's like to do an honest day's work. Most of 'em think manual labour's a Spanish museum. They're all fluff and no substance.' His unconvincing bluster actually makes me smile a little and I finally look over at him. 'Don't worry about me dad, I'll be fine. It might take me a while, but at the end of the day I'm a chip off the old block.'

There's a small silence. 'No,' he disagrees in a low tone that's completely out of character, 'You're not a chip off anything Victory Shackleford. You're much, much better than that. A one off. Noah Westbrook's made the biggest mistake of his life by listening to some muppet talk a load of codswallop.' He glares at me for a second as if daring me to argue, then abruptly pulls himself out of his chair. 'I have to go, got some business to attend to.' A couple of seconds later he's stomping down the stairs shouting back at Pickles to 'Get a bloody move on.' After a last lingering look towards Dotty, the old spaniel obediently trots after his master. The front door slams and quiet reigns.

Chapter Twenty One

As the Admiral climbed on board the passenger ferry to get him straight to Kingswear, he suddenly realized that he had no idea where Jimmy actually lived. He'd never been there - not once. He'd never even thought to ask where it was. Frowning, he sat on one of the seats inside the cabin, ignoring the inquisitive looks from the other passengers who were obviously up to speed with Dartmouth's biggest and most recent scandal. Pulling out his mobile phone, he looked up Jimmy's number, then hesitated, not at all sure if his friend would actually answer the phone if he called.

It abruptly dawned on him that Jimmy's request for permission to withdraw from the Ship Inn might not just have been from the pub, but actually from the Admiral's life altogether...

The sudden panic that gripped him was powerful and completely unexpected. Jimmy Noon was his oldest friend, and he couldn't imagine not having the small man in his life. He scowled at an unsuspecting passenger sitting opposite him. This was nothing less than mutiny, and simply couldn't be allowed to happen. There was only one way to put it right - if he could just find out where the old bastard bloody well lived.

In the end, the bird brained woman at Kingswear's small post office told him. Cost him a book of first class stamps and a box of envelopes for the information though. Damned audacity of the woman.

As he puffed and panted up the hill with Pickles wheezing

behind him, the Admiral went over exactly what he was going to say. He got as far as 'The thing is Jimmy lad,' when he suddenly realized that he'd arrived at his destination. He'd had no idea that Jimmy actually lived just round the corner from the Ship. In a gasping effort to get his breath back, he leaned against the door of his friend's house which turned out to be an immaculately maintained terrace, sporting a picturesque array of spring flowers overflowing a hanging basket and window box. After a few seconds of panting (both him and Pickles), and stalling (just him), he worked up the courage to knock on the door. This feeling of uncertainty and doubt was a completely new experience for Charles Shackleford. In fact, the last time he could remember being uncertain about anything was – well, never...

Taking a deep breath, he knocked again, uncertainty now being replaced with the much more familiar feeling of impatience. 'Where the bloody hell is everyone? How long does it actually take to answer a bollocking door?' he thought irritably, raising his hand to knock again, only to be suddenly faced with the poker face of Jimmy's wife Emily, who he hadn't seen for years. His first thought was, 'Bloody hell, she's got more chins than a Chinese phone book,' then, registering her less than friendly expression, he coughed slightly and asked if Jimmy was at home.

The annoying woman left him standing on the door step as she pursed her lips, and abruptly turned away without speaking. Still, she didn't shut the door in his face, and the Admiral was left feeling quietly confident, until he heard her shout from the depths of the house, 'Jim, the treacherous fossil's at the door.' Bloody cheek of the woman...

There was a pause of two or three minutes, while the Admiral attempted in his head to get past, 'The thing is, Jimmy lad,' then the small man appeared at the door, his face uncharacteristically solemn, giving nothing away. Any relief the Admiral was feeling promptly fled in the face of Jimmy's painfully formal and sombre expression, all his rehearsed words completely disintegrating into thin air. In the end, Charles Shackleford said simply, 'Jimmy lad, I've made a complete balls up. I know I'm about as welcome as a fart in a spacesuit right now, but I need you to come with me to London to help me put this cock up right. I swear to God it wasn't me said all that stuff. ' There was another pause as Jimmy's face remained unreadable, causing the Admiral to hold out his hand in an uncharacteristic plea. 'Please,' he muttered, the petition forced through his lips for probably the first time in forty years.

Jimmy stared at his former commanding officer for another couple of seconds, then he sighed and said, 'There's a train leaves for London Paddington at eight o'clock tomorrow morning, but we'll need to get to Totnes. I'll meet you at the taxi rank at seven.' As he turned away, intending to shut the door, the Admiral started to suggest that they take Jimmy's car to the station, but only got as far as 'Why can't,' before he saw the determined look on his friend's face, and closed his mouth with a snap. 'Good idea,' he mumbled instead, just before the door shut decisively in his face.

Looking down at Pickles, who was busy investigating something unrecognizable in the gutter, the Admiral exhaled noisily. 'Don't know what you think Pickles my boy, but I thought that went quite well. Now, let's see if you can bunk up with Mabel for the night.'

~*~

Charles Shackleford felt every painful second of the four hour train journey to London. Never had he been silent for so long. Although he'd agreed to accompany him, Jimmy spent the whole trip with his eyes closed, leaving the Admiral to stew in his own guilt, and agonize over exactly what he was going to say when he finally managed to track down Noah Westbrook. By the time the train pulled into Paddington Station, he'd drunk five cups of tea and three cups of coffee, purely for want of something to do. Now he wanted to pee so badly, he could swear his back teeth were floating.

After they exited the station, and stood at the taxi rank, Jimmy finally spoke. 'You have any idea where his hotel is Sir?' The Admiral glared at the smaller man, all thoughts of remorse temporarily forgotten, before sniffing and saying tetchily 'Bout time you said something. Was beginning to think nobody was home.

'No, I don't know where his hotel is, and couldn't very well ask Victory. I reckon they're filming in the Old Naval college at Greenwich, so I thought we'd grab one o' them water taxis from the embankment, and head down the river to see if we can collar him there. I know Greenwich of old, went there as a subby, so we should be able to sneak up on him before he gets wind of us and legs it.'

Jimmy frowned at the mental picture of Noah Westbrook doing a runner to escape from the wrath of Tory's vengeful father. 'More likely to be the other way round when he finds out what the Admiral's been up to,' he thought to himself wryly...

Two hours later, the two men disembarked from the water taxi at Greenwich under the gigantic shadow of the world famous Cutty Sark. Both the Admiral and Jimmy paused briefly to pay silent homage to one of the last surviving nineteenth century tea clippers. The fastest and greatest sailing ship of her time, it was now a museum attracting thousands of visitors from all over the world.

'Bloody tourists,' the Admiral muttered, as they fought their way through the throng of people surrounding the ship, and made their way towards the relatively sedate quiet of Greenwich Park.

Although most famous for Greenwich Mean Time, the world heritage site also housed the baroque splendour of the Old Royal Naval College, once a legendary bastion of British naval officer training, and now one of the top film locations in the UK. The Bridegroom was only the latest in a long line of movies filmed within its hallowed halls.

As they walked through the beautifully manicured grounds,

the Admiral glanced furtively around, looking for anybody he recognized, preferably without them recognizing him back. 'Reckon they're most likely to be filming in the Painted Hall,' he confided to Jimmy in a low whisper designed to thwart any nosy parkers listening in – even though the nearest person to them was at least fifty yards away. As Jimmy pointed this fact out, the Admiral gave an exasperated shake of his head at his friend's obtuseness.

'What the bloody hell's wrong with you Jimmy? he retorted in his usual condescending tone. 'I sometimes think you'd be out of your depth in a bloody car park puddle. You of all people should know that things aren't always what they seem on the surface...' Then suddenly remembering the importance of not upsetting his only ally, he clapped his friend on the back and continued hurriedly, 'But of course, I'm forgetting you don't have my experience in matters of British Intelligence, so we'll say no more on the matter.' Striding away, he didn't notice Jimmy's narrowed eyes and tight lips, and thus had no inkling that his relationship with his oldest friend was on the brink of changing – perhaps not radically, after all, there was rank etiquette to maintain – but no longer would Jimmy follow his hero blindly. He'd said as much to Emily, and actually her response had been quite gratifying…

Feeling somewhat mollified, Jimmy hurried after the Admiral, who was now skulking behind one of the stone pillars about twenty yards away from the porticoed entrance to the Painted Hall, currently cordoned off from the public. A small crowd of mostly women gathered outside the barricade suggested they'd probably come to the right place, and, nodding his head towards the grand doorway, the Admiral pointed at Jimmy, indicating the smaller man should go and check it out. 'Why me Sir?' Jimmy's response was a heated whisper causing the Admiral to sigh at his friend's continued dim-wittedness. 'Less likely to recognize you,' he responded in a low tone, then aiming for a note of encouragement, 'Come on Jimmy lad, it's just like old times…'

Rolling his eyes, Jimmy nevertheless allowed himself to be shoved unceremoniously out of their hiding place, and, making an effort to look inconspicuous, walked nonchalantly towards the small crowd hovering around the cordoned entrance. Five minutes later he was back. 'They're definitely in there,' he said without bothering to lower his voice this time. 'Apparently they're filming in the Upper Hall. Been there all morning.'

The Admiral frowned at this news, glancing back at the crowd waiting patiently to see their idols. 'Well we can't wait here,' he said finally. 'We won't even get a look in with this bloody lot.'

Both men fell silent for a few minutes, pondering their next move. 'What about the car?' blurted Jimmy suddenly, grasping the Admiral's arm in excitement. He won't have walked here that's for sure. We'll nab him just as he gets in the car.' The Admiral opened his mouth to make an objection, but closed it again when he couldn't find anything to disagree with. It was risky, but what else were they going to do?

They took it in turns to pop over to the toilets in the Visitor Centre, keeping their mobile phones handy in case of any sudden action. After two hours, Jimmy declared he was bloody starving and announced he was off to get them both some scran, almost giving the Admiral a coronary by going off without requesting permission. For the first time, Charles Shackleford felt the chill winds of change coming. Still, he couldn't deny the ham sandwich definitely hit the spot.

After another half an hour of inaction, there was a sudden flurry of activity near the Hall entrance as a sleek black limousine drove slowly up from the East Gate. 'Come on Jimmy lad, we're on,' shouted the Admiral, stealth obviously gone out of the window in his haste to get into position. The group of fans surged towards the car from the back, as the Admiral and Jimmy rushed forward to the front, and they spent precious seconds jostling for the position closest to the rear door facing the entrance.

Two minutes and a potential black eye later, the doors to the Painted Hall opened, and out walked Noah Westbrook accompanied by what looked like two security types. The Admiral's heart sank. He knew it, he was buggered. He'd never get near the actor now. He had seconds to come up with a plan before Noah spotted him. Unfortunately, for once in his life, his mind was a total blank, and grinding his teeth in frustration, the Admiral waited, knowing the exact moment Noah's eyes fastened on him in recognition. Stopping, the actor turned to speak in a low voice to one of his companions and the Admiral realized it was now or never. Grabbing hold of a startled Jimmy, he leaned against the small man and groaned loudly.

Unfortunately, the excited chatter of the fans drowned his efforts and he knew the situation called for more drastic action. 'For Victory,' he mumbled to himself before stepping forward and keeling over, practically at Noah Westbrook's feet, in what appeared to be either a dead faint or just plain dead...

Lying face down on the gravel, the Admiral could hear the slightly panicked squeals as individuals backed off from his prostrate body, and, resisting the urge to chuckle, he let out a convincing moan. For a few heart stopping seconds nothing happened, until eventually any inclination to snigger disappeared with the realization there was a distinct possibility Noah was going to simply step over him to get to the car. Hurriedly he let out a louder, more theatrical groan and to his relief, a pair of shoes appeared next to his head.

'Well Admiral,' drawled a familiar voice in his ear, 'Your family obviously has a predilection for throwing yourselves at my feet.' The Admiral had no idea what Noah was talking about, so instead of attempting to speak, he opted for a credible whimper, wishing that the man would get a bloody move on and help him to his feet - it was damn cold on this stone. Sighing, Noah rose from his crouch, and a couple of seconds later hands lifted him non too gently up from the floor and helped him into the back seat of the limousine. He risked a quick wink at Jimmy who was staring in open mouthed amazement at the Admiral's performance, then the door shut. Closing his eyes, he leaned his head back with an exaggerated sigh, just as Noah climbed in from the other side.

'You can cut the melodramatics now Admiral,' came Noah's dry voice as they pulled away. 'I'll have the driver drop you off at the nearest tube station.'

The Admiral opened his eyes quickly, recognizing he only had minutes at best to plead Victory's case. Glancing over at Noah's stony expression, he took a deep breath and dropped his act. He still had no idea how he was going to convince Noah of his daughter's innocence in the whole sordid affair. The only thing he knew for certain was that he was going to have to come clean about his own involvement. Unfortunately, coming clean about anything was not one of Charles Shackleford's strong points...

In the end it took him forty five minutes to convince Noah that Tory had known nothing about the newspaper article, and the Admiral had no doubt about the exact second the actor finally believed him. The relief in Noah's face was palpable.

'I swear all I did was give the bloody reporter a couple of hints about you and Victory,' he finished finally. 'I just wanted to give you a bit of a nudge in the right direction. Didn't want Tory left high and dry after you'd finished with her.'

'What, like now you mean?' Noah interrupted coldly. The Admiral ducked his head in acknowledgement of his own stupidity before continuing, 'I didn't know anything about the other stuff lad. I've no bloody idea where he got his information from – I just know it weren't my Victory.'

There was silence for a few minutes as Noah processed everything the Admiral had told him. 'So how did you get the name of this reporter?' he asked eventually.

The Admiral paused before he answered, a horrible sick feeling in the pit of his stomach that for once wasn't over indulgence.

'It was Gaynor Andrews. She gave me the number.'

Chapter Twenty Two

I can't believe it's the beginning of July already and a whole month since my world fell apart. Well maybe that's a tad overdramatic but believe me, if misery had a name, it would be Tory Shackleford. The only slight positive in the whole hideous situation is that I've lost a few pounds. I've been trying so hard to keep myself busy and I'm gradually getting to the point where I can go a whole ten minutes without thinking about Noah. Luckily The Bridegroom isn't coming out until next year and I'm really hoping my broken heart will have at least sorted out a patch up job by then.

You see, positive thinking...

The paparazzi camped outside the Admiralty gave up after a couple of weeks, since they couldn't track me down and both Noah and Gaynor steadfastly refused to comment. Oh they made up a few things, got the odd friend of a friend of a friend to share a couple of colourful, though mostly bullshit, anecdotes, but there's only so long a story can run when there really is nothing new to add to it.

So here I am, life back to normal. I've not seen much of my father. I think broken-hearted daughters are not really his thing. I know he doesn't know what to say to me, spends most of his time tiptoeing around the house like somebody's died. It's actually so far from my father's normal behaviour, it's downright creepy. So, to help him out, I've been spending as much time as I can at the gallery - when I'm not out and about costing up some really amazing design projects. Seems notoriety is not always a bad thing because business has never been so good...

Today's Sunday, so there's no hurry to get started. Dotty and I are taking our time, opting for a pleasant stroll instead the usual sprint down the garden to grab the ferry on its way over. To be fair, the strolling bit is me – Dotty is doing her usual mad dash up and down, barking at anything with a pulse. Noisy though she is, I can't help but smile. The little dog has been my lifeline over the last few weeks. I really don't know what I'd have done without her, Kit and Freddy.

As we exit the garden near the ferry slipway, I put Dotty on her leash, noting the queue of cars waiting to cross over the river is getting longer as the summer progresses. It'll soon be impossible to park anywhere in Dartmouth.

Dotty starts trembling the second the ferry arrives and I pick her up while I walk up the slipway, avoiding the cars filing slowly past us as they board. As the ferry moves away from the shore, I lean against the railing, Dotty securely in my arms, and watch the hive of activity up and down the Dart. It's a beautiful summer day and it seems nearly everyone and his dog is out on the water. I can't help but wish I'd had the time to take Noah sailing. I imagine us heading up the river to the Anchorstone café situated right on the edge of the river Dart in the tiny village of Dittisham. Today would have been perfect for an al fresco seafood lunch. I picture us sharing a bottle of wine on the outside terrace overlooking the water. Noah would have loved it. I can see his laughing face so clearly in my head that an unexpected wave of longing hits me - so intense that I almost want to scream. Turning away from the picturesque view, I stumble to a seat and sit, blinking back the tears that threaten to swamp me. 'For God sake get a grip girl,' I mumble to myself, taking a deep breath as I realize we've reached the other side. Hurriedly I disembark and walk quickly towards the town centre, all thoughts of a slow leisurely start now overtaken by the need to hide away in my office sanctuary.

The gallery door is open for business when I arrive, but, to my dismay, the inside is packed with holiday makers. Sighing, I pick Dotty up again, and mumbling 'Excuse me,' I squeeze carefully past the largely oblivious visitors. As I weave my way through, I spot Kit at the other side of the shop and give her a cursory wave without stopping, determined to reach my refuge before I humiliate myself by bursting into tears. As I finally pause to put Dotty down in front of the office door, I realize with surprise that it's shut, and, frowning slightly, I give it an experimental shove, breathing a small sigh of relief to find it unlocked. Before I have chance to open it properly, I hear Kit call my name urgently and glance back to give her a reassuring smile and return her wave. The poor love is still so protective of me. Then, completely unaware of the frantic war dance she's doing behind my back, I turn and push the door open the rest of the way.

Where Noah Westbrook is sitting waiting for me.

I stop just inside the door, heart hammering in my chest as I watch him slowly rise from the chair. I have absolutely no idea what to do. Dotty of course has no such inhibitions and throws herself at him barking joyfully. As he bends down to fuss the little dog, I remain rooted to the spot, staring silently at the face that has haunted my dreams, waking and sleeping, for the past month. Then he straightens up and stares back at me.

'Why are you here?' I whisper finally, unable to stop the tears from coursing down my cheeks.

Seeing my distress, he takes a step towards me, and I back up, holding out my hand to ward him away. 'Why are you here?' I ask again, my voice cracking.

He closes his eyes briefly and takes a deep breath. Then, 'I'm here to tell you how sorry I am,' he murmurs softly, achingly, his incredible eyes never leaving mine. 'I'm here to ask you to forgive me. I know it wasn't you who leaked the story to the press. I have no excuse for the way I've treated you except to say it's so damn easy to believe the worst of everyone in this business, even when it's someone I'd trust with my life.'

I shake my head in disbelief at his words, at his gentle tone, after the cold expressionless man I'd seen in London.

Shuddering, I wrap my arms around my middle and continue to stare at him wordlessly.

Groaning, he runs his fingers through his hair. 'I love you Tory.' His voice this time is harsh with emotion and need. 'I didn't know what love was until you came into my life. I want to spend the rest of my life loving you. I...' He pauses, closing his eyes briefly, before pleading, his voice now almost a whisper. 'Please Tory.'

I gaze silently at him for a few more seconds, taking in his clenched hands and anguished face and I realize that incredibly, unbelievably, everything he's saying is true. Noah Westbrook is in love with me.

And he doesn't expect me to believe him.

Taking a deep breath, I relax, allowing my arms to drop by my side, all the while holding his tormented gaze. 'I love you too,' I say simply, quietly. 'I have since the first moment I saw you.'

As soon as the words leave my mouth, he strides forward to pull me unresisting into his arms. Holding me tight, he tracks kisses from my head to my ear, his velvety voice like a heated caress over my skin, then his lips find mine, hot, demanding and I stop thinking altogether.

When Kit finally ventures into the office twenty minutes later, I'm firmly ensconced in Noah's lap. I was a bit worried at first that he'd need resuscitating if I sat on him too long, but since he's holding me like he has no intention of ever letting me go, I've decided to give in and relax...

Definitely lost a few pounds.

~*~

Turns out that the whole story was leaked by Gaynor. Apparently she got the idea when my father drunkenly confided his fears about my relationship with Noah to her on the night of the music festival. She agreed that he should put out a few hints to the press and gave him the number of a reporter who owed her a favour. She then anonymously added to my father's relatively humdrum information with a story that the press would kill to get hold of...

Why? Noah says he doesn't know. He can't understand why on earth she would want the public to know something so private. Apparently as soon as Noah confronted her, she collapsed in floods of tears and told him she'd been tricked into giving the information.

As to the why? I think I know the answer. Gaynor Andrews is still in love with Noah and she believed it was only a matter of time until they got back together. When Noah admitted to her that he'd confided in me, she realized just how serious things were between us and thought she was on the verge of losing him forever. I think she hoped that by revealing the story to the whole world in a way that would garner public sympathy, and by putting the blame for the leak on me, it would split us up and throw the two of them together. In her eyes, it was the only way she stood a chance of getting him back.

I don't suppose I'll ever know the whole truth. Gaynor has flown back to the States to lick her wounds. She'll need to return to the UK in a few weeks to finish filming The Bridegroom, but that's a problem for another day.

Today I've found out that Noah Westbrook loves me. Who knows what tomorrow will bring, but I'm living proof that dreams can and do come true and I'm grabbing hold of mine with both hands.

I just know it's going to be an amazing ride.

Chapter Twenty Three

The limousine is cruising slowly through the crowds gathered outside the Empire Cinema in Leicester Square. The July evening is warm and sultry, perfect for the hundreds of fans waiting patiently to see their screen idols at the British Premier of The Bridegroom.

My stomach is doing somersaults and I desperately need to go to the bathroom. Not that I'm going to be able to any time soon. The red strapless taffeta evening gown I've been poured into has definitely put paid to that. I look over at Noah sitting opposite me, magnificent in full evening dress and can't help but think what the hell is this gorgeous person doing with me? Then he takes my hand with a smile and I see the love in his beautiful eyes and all of a sudden my nerves disappear. I smile back just as the car slows to a stop at the red carpet.

'Well here we go then, sooner we get the boring bit over, the sooner we can head off for the shindig after.' I look in exasperation at my father, resplendent in his mess undress that unfortunately smells of mothballs to anyone getting too close. 'Please dad, don't embarrass me tonight okay?' He looks at me in complete surprise as though he couldn't believe I'd even contemplate such a thing. He's about to speak but then the door opens, and whatever he was going to say is lost.

Noah gets out of the car first and I hear the increased roar of the crowds as they spot him. I watch furtively through the tinted window as he waves calmly to the surging throng. Then he leans back into the car and holds out his hand for me to join him. Taking a deep breath, heart thundering in my chest, I step out into the warm night. There's a brief pause as I straighten my dress and we wait for the Admiral to disentangle his braces from his seatbelt, then, secure in the knowledge that nothing awful can happen as long as my dad remains right behind me, we begin our slow procession along the red carpet towards the cinema entrance. Noah is completely relaxed as he stops to make brief conversation with fans trying to get his attention. This is his world and I'm content simply to hover next to him in smiling silence, my hand held securely in his.

Until, all of a sudden I realize my father's missing. Frantically I turn round and spot him talking to a presenter from E! Entertainment. My heart plummets to my Jimmy Choos and I feel the oh so familiar sense of impending doom as he begins to speak.

'Well it has to be said my Victory's not the sharpest knife in the drawer and, to be fair, she can be a bit of a social hand grenade, but apart from that, well you'd have to be a complete knob jockey not to realize that they're absolutely perfect for each other.'

I freeze in embarrassment and glance up at Noah, only to find him grinning down at me in unadulterated delight.

'Your father really is an absolute treasure,' he murmurs in my ear. 'I just knew he wouldn't let us down. Shall we go in?'

THE END

Do you want to find out why the most famous film star in the world fell for an ordinary girl?

Falling For Victory tells the story of Claiming Victory from Noah's point of view. Find out how and why he fell in love with Tory...

Sign up to my newsletter by copying and pasting the link below and I'll send you a FREE ebook copy of Falling For Victory

https://motivated-teacher-3299.ck.page/d68eed985f

Also, if you enjoyed Claiming Victory, you may be interested to know that Book Two: *Sweet Victory*, Book Three: *All For Victory*, Book Four: *Chasing Victory* and Book Five: *Lasting Victory* - are all available on Amazon.

If you'd like a taster of *Sweet Victory,* keep reading for an exclusive sneak peek...

Sweet Victory

Chapter One

It was just over a year since Hollywood had descended on the small yachting haven of Dartmouth and after all the excitement, things had very much returned to normal.

In fact, as far as Admiral Charles Shackleford (Retired) was concerned, nothing had changed at all. Except for one thing ...

Ensconced on his favourite bar stool in the Ship Inn, he sighed irritably, and stared down into his pint. Where the bloody hell was Jimmy?

Since the shenanigans in London, his best friend had had a right wendy on. In fact, though he would never admit it to a soul, the Admiral would almost have given away his beloved Admiralty to have things the way they used to be. He sighed again, this time bemoaning things lost. His former Master At Arms had got a taste of freedom and wasn't likely to be put back in his box any time soon. Of course it was all down to that dragon Jimmy lived with, and nothing at all to do with a certain retired officer interfering in affairs that were none of his concern.

Sighing for the third time, Charles Shackleford reflected on the ungratefulness of people. After all, it had all turned out toppers in the end.

Except for the fact that nothing else had changed. Victory was still living at home – most of the time, when she wasn't up to her elbows in builder's dust up at Noah's place. But the Yank still hadn't popped the question. The Admiral frowned. He thought he could just move Tory out and Mabel in. Problem was, it wasn't turning out to be quite so simple. Mabel wanted him to make an honest woman of her. Flatly refused to leave her cosy cottage for his "mausoleum" unless she had a ring on her finger.

Now he wasn't averse to marrying Mabel – she was a much better cook than Victory – but how could he possibly have a wedding before his own daughter?

And that was the crux of the matter. Although it grieved him to admit it, he needed to ask Jimmy's advice – except that his friend had gone decidedly lily livered since that slight hiccup with Victory and Noah last year.

Suddenly the door to the Ship opened, bringing with it a blast of fresh air, and, much to the Admiral's relief, the small figure of Jimmy – along with Pickles who had apparently been sitting patiently outside in the porch for the last twenty minutes.

'Sorry I'm late Sir,' Jimmy breathed, hurriedly divesting himself of his coat on the way to the bar. 'Had a few things to do with Emily this morning.'

Admiral Shackleford resisted the urge to ask exactly what could be more important than their Friday lunch time drink - mostly because he was actually worried that Jimmy might tell him. He contented himself with a frown and a slight sniff. At least his friend hadn't gone completely AWOL, and still understood the importance of recognizing rank.

Signalling to the barmaid to bring another pint for himself and one for Jimmy, the Admiral waited impatiently for the smaller man to climb onto his bar stool and get settled. In the end, his impatience got the better of him. 'What the bloody hell are you doing Jimmy?' he demanded irritably, as Jimmy continued to shuffle his bottom. 'You look like a trained monkey.'

Glancing up at his friend's crotchety face, Jimmy nevertheless persisted with his fidgeting, until eventually, settled to his satisfaction, he leaned forward and picked his beer up from the bar. 'Got the stool with the rip in,' he finally responded mildly before taking a long draft of his pint.

The Admiral had never wanted to turn the clock back more than at that particular moment. A year ago, such an offhand comment would have resulted in Jimmy doing four days dishwasher duty. That bloody woman he was married to had a lot to answer for. Taking a hasty swallow of his own beer, the Admiral stemmed his rising frustration, reminding himself that he needed his friend's help.

Placing his pint decisively back on the bar, the Admiral took a deep breath. 'The thing is Jimmy lad, I've got a bit of a situation and, even though you're usually as much use as tits on a bull, it has to be said that two brains focusing on the problem are much better than one.'

Jimmy put his own drink back on the bar and turned towards the Admiral with a frown. What the hell had the silly bugger got himself involved in now? He was tempted to tell the conniving old shark exactly what he could do with his situation, but at the end of the day, old habits really do die hard, and, as much as he'd promised Emily that he wouldn't get drawn into to any more of the Admiral's harebrained schemes, he heard himself saying, 'What can I do for you Sir?'

'That's the spirit Jimmy,' the Admiral responded enthusiastically, causing Jimmy's heart to plummet in alarm. 'See, even though I was selflessly instrumental in bringing Noah and Victory together…' Jimmy's look of complete incredulity caused him to falter slightly, but after a short pause, he coughed and ploughed on determinedly, '…it occurred to me that they are not yet *exactly* together.' He halted expectantly, waiting for Jimmy to acknowledge his superior observational skills. Instead he watched his friend go an interesting shade of purple while making peculiar strangling sounds.

Just when as he was about to ask if the cat had got his tongue, the Admiral jumped as Jimmy leaped off the stool shouting, 'Are you out of your mi…?' only to be cut off as he landed straight on top of Pickles' tail. The elderly Springer, who'd been dozing contentedly at their feet, took off like a sprightly two year old, leaving Jimmy pole axed at Charles Shackleford's feet.

Ignoring his dog who was now sitting shivering behind the bar, the Admiral stared down in astonishment at his friend lying stunned in front of him. 'What the bollocking hell's wrong with you today man, you're acting like a lost fart in a haunted milk bottle. Have you been on the hard stuff?'

Staring up at the red veined face directly above him, Jimmy opened his mouth but nothing came out. It had to be said, he actually felt a bit light headed – not surprising really as he'd cracked his head on the edge of the stool on his way down. Gingerly feeling around the back of his skull for a lump, he managed to sit up with absolutely no help from the Admiral who was still staring at him as though he were a particularly bizarre form of aquatic life.

Finally staggering to his feet, Jimmy clambered shakily back onto his stool while trying to gather his scattered wits together. Charles Shackleford shook his head at his friend's apparent clumsiness as he handed him his pint with a nod towards its amber contents. 'Drink that lad, it'll put you back on your feet. Can't think what's got into you today. Lucky the pub's not full. PICKLES...' The last was shouted at the top of his voice causing Jimmy to wince and close his eyes. Appearing round the corner of the bar looking sheepish but none the worse for wear, Pickles gingerly returned to his earlier spot, keeping a wary eye out for any further falling limbs.

'So Jimmy boy,' the Admiral continued, completely dismissing his friend's recent brush with possible death or at least the odd broken bone, 'Bottom line is I want to marry Mabel but can't do it while our Victory's still not hitched. What do you think? I'm counting on you. In the words of Black Adder, we need to come up with a plan so cunning you could stick a tail on it and call it a fox...'

Chapter Two

'Hang on a minute Dotty, I'll be with you in a couple of seconds, just don't christen the fifteen thousand pound Persian rug in the meantime.' Hurriedly I finish attaching the last hook onto the curtain rail and clamber down the step ladder to let the little dog out into the garden. Smiling, I watch her immediately dash off in a flurry of excited barking towards a particularly large crow sitting eyeing her disdainfully from the fence. Then, as she disappears from view, I turn back to survey my handiwork.

Fourteen months, one week and three days after starting this project, Noah's house is finally beginning to look like a home. I've just finished hanging the last of the curtains up to the enormous bi-fold doors leading out onto the newly constructed porch and terrace beyond, and, though I say so myself, the room really is beautiful. Decorated in soft pastel blues and greys so reminiscent of the British seaside, the drawing room seems to echo the ever changing moods of the ocean. It hardly resembles the one I sat in so many months ago while trying to convince Noah Westbrook, aka gorgeous Hollywood superstar, to let me be his decorator. Taking a chance on an unknown is typical of the enigma that is Noah. And, of course, falling in love with one is too.

Sighing I pick up the step ladders and take them into the utility room. My arms are aching after holding heavy fabric in the air for so long and I rub them absently as I wander back into the bright shiny state of the art kitchen.

The last year has been an amazing roller coaster. Working on the house in between travelling to see Noah on location as he finished filming *The Bridegroom*, dodging the paparazzi, and culminating in the premier in Leicester Square. The film has been a huge success, helping to cement Noah's status as the most in demand actor in the world.

The problem is, I don't know where that leaves me. His house is practically finished. His house. I don't need a ring, I really don't, but it's difficult loving someone who everyone wants a piece of, especially when I can in no way compete. I know I sound whiny, ungrateful, not to mention downright pathetic, and when Noah and I are together, everything is fine.

It's when we're apart that the uncertainties rear their ugly heads, and right now, that's most of the time. I haven't actually seen Noah since the premier nearly six weeks ago. He's off filming his latest blockbuster – a sci-fi thriller. Still, apparently they're going to be on location in Ireland over the next few weeks, so at least we'll only have the Irish sea separating us and hopefully we might grab some private time together.

Dotty's barking and scratching at the door pulls me out of my maudlin reverie and I make a concerted effort to pull myself together as I go to let her back in. Live for the present, I tell myself sternly and stop analyzing everything to the nth degree...

As I open the door, my mobile phone rings, and looking down I smile as Kit's name comes up on the screen. I haven't seen my best friend for over a week as she's been off on one of her buying trips for the gallery.

'Hey Kitty Kat, how's it going, you back?' I ask closing the door as Dotty comes shooting in.

'Yeah, home safe and sound,' she responds, 'I cut the trip short to get back into Dartmouth before the madness of Regatta week and no parking spaces within a ten mile radius.' She pauses, then goes on carefully, 'Will Noah be coming back for the Regatta?'

'Doubtful,' is my glum response.

'Then we'll just have to party without him.' Kit's tone as always pulls me out of my down in the dumps mood and I can't help but picture the mischief we've got up to in previous regattas over the years.

Dartmouth Royal Regatta Sailing week is arguably one of the UK's oldest sailing regattas. It's definitely one of the most popular and the town is usually crammed throughout the week for the various on shore and off shore entertainment. Basically, a whole week of total chaos...

Smiling, I ask if she's crewing for Ben Sheppherd this year.

'Don't think so, haven't seen him for a while. Not even sure he's racing this year. Rumour has it he's split up with his wife and taking it pretty bad.'

'Wow, bummer. I thought they were really good together. He

absolutely idolized her. If you see him, tell him how sorry I am.' Then, determinedly changing the subject from couples splitting up, 'So, how did the shopping go?'

'Pretty successful, I managed to bag some nice goodies for the lead up to Christmas. Just don't like thinking about it in August.'

'Hear, hear,' I respond resolutely refusing to think about Christmas and exactly where Noah and I will be then.

'You fancy exchanging your ivory palace in progress for the cosy delights of the Cherub and a bottle of wine?' As usual Kit immediately senses my anxiety and takes the best possible steps to alleviate it. What on earth would I do without her?

'Sounds good.' I smile down the phone before glancing down at my watch and adding, 'Early doors?'

'Perfect, see you there at six. We'll discuss our plans for the Regatta. It's only two weeks away. Me thinks we might need some chips, you know, added brain power...'

Laughing I put down the phone, my good humour restored. 'Come on Dotspot, our shift's over for the day.' Dotty looks up from her frenzied back scratching on said fifteen thousand pound rug, before rolling over and doing a bit of enthusiastic digging. I can't help but wince a little as I hurriedly pick her up. Good job Noah's not too house proud.

After checking everything's okay, I set the alarm before heading out of the front door. As I walk towards my car parked a little way down the narrow road, I pause and turn back to view the small section of Noah's house that's visible from the road. It really is a hidden gem. To anyone passing, it appears to be a small bungalow set on the side of the road, but that impression is completely misleading. The vast majority of the house is completely concealed from the road and is set into the hillside with its garden stretching down towards the beautiful River Dart.

Turning back to my car, I unlock the door and put Dotty on the back seat. As I make my way round to the driver's side, her sudden excited barking makes me jump and I look up to see a familiar figure making his way from under some trees down the road.

Sighing, I lean back against the driver's door. 'Hello Harry, how long have you been lurking in the bushes?'

'Not long,' comes the cheerful reply, 'Only a couple of hours.'

'You do know that Noah's not here don't you?' Harry freelances for one of the more lurid tabloids, but unlike most of the paparazzi, he actually seems nice. We've had several in depth discussions about the sorry state of journalism today and most of the pictures he's taken of me have actually been quite flattering – in fact I think he might even have airbrushed a couple...

'I know. He's on his way to Al Massira airport in Morocco as we speak,' he responds with a dismissive wave of his hand. I shake my head ruefully in recognition that the small man knows more about my beloved's whereabouts than I do. 'It's actually you I wanted to speak to.' I frown at the unaccustomed seriousness in his voice and my heart thuds painfully in my chest.

I resist the urge to jump in the car and drive away as something in his tone tells me I don't really want to hear what he has to say. Instead I offer him a lift down into Kingswear, my heart beating faster as he nods his head solemnly and walks round to the passenger side without saying anything else.

For the next few moments, the only sound in the car is me as I start the engine, and Dotty as she throws herself joyfully into Harry's lap. That's another reason why I like him. Dotty's a very good judge of character. As I wind my way carefully down the road towards Kingswear, I risk glancing over at him, just as he raises his head to look over at me. This time my heart lurches sickeningly as I witness the sympathy in his gaze.

Not again, please, please, not again.

I turn my eyes determinedly back to the road as I wait for him to tell me that Noah has been caught in a compromising position with one of the bevy of beautiful women that hover around him like bees round a honey pot. To my surprise, his first words aren't about Noah at all. 'Word on the streets is they've dug up some dirt on your old man.' I pull a face as his words sink in.

'What, like he was possibly the worst two star ever to grace the Royal Navy's wall of fame? I think that's common knowledge sunshine.'

'Trust me Tory, it's much worse than that. God knows how, but they've unearthed a retired Thai prostitute who says your father murdered her husband.

I'm on my second glass of wine and I'm only now beginning to calm down. Harry didn't know the full story, only that the incident allegedly happened when my father was a lowly Lieutenant.

After dropping Harry off at the Passenger Ferry in Kingswear, I drove round to the Admiralty like I was auditioning for Brands Hatch, but there was no sign of my father, or Pickles for that matter. I tried his mobile phone but like always, it was switched off. In the end, I called Kit to tell her that I wasn't feeling well and wouldn't be coming over to the Cherub, poured myself a large glass of wine, and sat down in his study to wait. My mind is now racing. How on earth could my bluff, big hearted, irresponsible father possibly have murdered anybody? God knows I've been tempted to do him in myself a few times. Un-PC he might be, but a murderer, never. And what the hell was he doing getting involved with a Thai prostitute (well obviously I *do* know, but still...) And anyway wasn't he with mum by the time he joined the Royal Navy... Oh God, I'm just going round in circles. I daren't even think about how this is going to affect Noah.

Suddenly my endless head chatter is interrupted by the sound of a door opening. I know it's the Admiral because Dotty is beside herself with happiness (at seeing Pickles, not my father...) I stand nervously, gripping my half empty glass like a lifeline and wait for him to open the study door.

'Victory,' he shouts as he stomps across the hall, obviously nearly falling over Pickles in the process if the sudden crash and, 'Bloody hell dog, you'll have me arse over tit in a minute,' is anything to go by. 'Vict....' He stutters to a halt as he throws open the study door and sees me standing there. It's so unusual for him to find me in his personal sanctuary that for a couple of seconds he's actually lost for words. Then, taking in my white face and stiff posture, he turns and closes the door before saying in an uncharacteristically mild tone, 'Do I need a drop of the hard stuff before we start?'

I nod, not trusting myself to speak. I can tell he thinks this is all about Noah. He has absolutely no idea of the bombshell I'm about to drop. I sit down and try to compose myself as he helps himself to a glass of port. Even Dotty and Pickles sense that something is wrong as they sit side by side on the rug and stare anxiously at us both.

'Right then.' His voice is matter of fact as he plonks himself in his chair opposite. 'Come on girl, spit it out. Has the Yank dumped you or what?'

I shake my head, for once completely oblivious to his less than gentle method of questioning. 'No, well, not yet anyway.' I hold my hand up as he tries to interrupt, and continue breathlessly, 'It's not about Noah dad. It's about you.' At his frown, I take a large gulp of my wine and finish in a rush, 'Dad they're saying you killed a Thai prostitute, well not a prostitute exactly, but the husband of one. You didn't did you? You couldn't possibly have done something like that could you? I mean what were you doing in Thailand and why would you have anything to do with a prostitute, or the husband of one? Weren't you and mum married by then?' I splutter to a halt, the sick feeling intensifying in my stomach as I take in his stillness and sudden pallor.

The silence lengthens. 'Dad?' I whisper, fear clogging my throat at his failure to answer. 'Please dad, you have to talk to me. It's going to be all over the news by the weekend.' For a few more seconds, I actually think he's not going to answer and I have to resist the urge to get up and shake him. Then he sighs and closes his eyes briefly before swallowing his glass of port in one go.

Finally he looks across at me. 'I didn't kill anyone Victory, nobody did. It was an accident.' And, despite my best efforts, he refuses to say another word.

Daylight is beginning to fade into dusk outside as dad and I continue to sit in silence. According to Harry, the story will break in the next couple of days, and I want to scream and shout at my father, beg him to come clean and tell the world what really happened, but I know how he works. Begging and pleading will get me nowhere. So instead I do nothing, simply stare into my now empty glass and wish I could drown my sorrows in the rest of the bottle.

'I need to speak to Jimmy.' His sudden announcement makes me jump and I look up as he stands to fish his mobile phone out of his pocket. 'Why,' I ask bluntly, 'Is he involved in this mess too?' My father's answer is to raise his eyebrows and frown at me until sighing, I climb reluctantly out of my chair and turn on the lamps. I need to speak to Noah too, as soon as possible. Trouble is, I can't bring myself to do it just yet. I have no idea what he'll say. Leaving dad to his phone call, I head to the kitchen to sort out dog food and make some sandwiches - mostly as something solid to soak up the wine (the sandwiches that is, not the dog food...)

My mind stays blessedly numb as I focus determinedly on the mundane actions of spreading and cutting, and when my father pushes open the kitchen door ten minutes later, I'm surprised to note that I've used up nearly a whole loaf of bread. 'Bollocking hell Victory, we might have a bit of a problem, but we're not on the verge of a bloody famine.' I stare down at the knife in my hand and grit my teeth. A bit of a problem? I'll give him a bit of a problem...

Leaning down to grab one of the sandwiches, my father waves it at me before taking a large appreciative bite, completely oblivious to my murderous thoughts. 'Everything's going to be shipshape Victory, don't you worry. Thing is, they can't prove anything.' The breadcrumbs spraying everywhere are the least of my worries as I stare incredulously at him. 'Nobody was done in, it's all just a big misunderstanding. All we need to do is lie low for a bit and it'll all blow over, you'll see.'

Obviously my completely deluded parent has recovered from his brief spell of vulnerability and is now firmly back in cloud cuckoo land. 'Dad, they are going to hang you out to dry. Can't you see that?' My voice has risen to a shout and I take a deep breath in an effort to calm down. 'The police will want to question you,' I continue more evenly. 'You won't be able to lie low anywhere. You could even go to prison. We're talking about a murder dad, not just a one day wonder of an ex-Admiral shagging a hooker forty years ago…'

He sighs, looking for all the world as though I'm the problem. 'You don't need to worry,' he says again, slowly this time. 'I'll turn myself in, they'll let me out on bail and then we'll hole up somewhere quiet until it's all sorted.' I gawp at him in complete disbelief at his naivety. 'So what exactly are you going to say happened dad? How are you going to explain it? You said it was an accident.'

'Aye, it was,' he responds firmly. 'But I won't be breathing a word of what happened to you or anyone else.' Then he glares at me with uncharacteristic steel and, for the first time ever, I see a glimmer of the qualities that got him promoted to Admiral. 'I'll sort this bloody mess out Victory and I don't want you involved. I mean it, you leave this to me. If you so much as stick your little toe into this mess, I will no longer call you my daughter. And with that he grabs another sandwich, calls to Pickles and disappears out of the door.

Sweet Victory is available from Amazon in ebook and paperback

Author's Note

The beautiful yachting haven of Dartmouth in South Devon holds a very special place in my heart – not least because I met my husband there :-)

If you're ever in the area, please take the time out to visit. The pubs and restaurants I describe are real and I've spent many a happy lunchtime/evening in each of them. The Anchorstone café at Dittisham is also a must for anyone who loves alfresco dining and sea food.

If you'd like more information about Dartmouth and the surrounding areas, here's a link to the Tourist Information Centre. Simply copy and paste into your browser.

https://discoverdartmouth.com

To all you Dartmothians out there, I know I missed off the Steam Railway - it was deliberate and I hope you'll forgive me. It just made things too complicated to include…

Greenwich World Heritage Site in London is also another amazing place to visit if you're ever in the Capital. The site houses The National Maritime Museum, The Queens House, The Royal Observatory, The Cutty Sark and The Old Royal Naval College. The Painted Hall in Claiming Victory is part of the Old Naval College. Designed by Sir Christopher Wren, it is absolutely breathtaking, and with its exuberant wall and ceiling decorations, is often described as the finest dining hall in Europe.

For more information visit:

http://www.visitgreenwich.org.uk/

It's also quite true that The Old Royal Naval College at Greenwich has been host to many big screen blockbusters and TV dramas, including Four Weddings and a Funeral, Sense and Sensibility, The Queen, Skyfall, The Kings Speech and Les Miserables.

Keeping in Touch

Thank you so much for reading *Claiming Victory*, I really hope you enjoyed it.

For any of you who'd like to connect, I'd really love to hear from you. Feel free to contact me via my facebook page at https://www.facebook.com/beverleywattsauthor

If you'd like me to let you know as soon as my next book is available and receive your free ebook - Falling For Victory - sign up to my newsletter and I'll send you the ebook and keep you updated about all my latest releases.

https://motivated-teacher-3299.ck.page/143a008c18

And lastly, thanks a million for taking the time to read this story. If you've not yet had your fill of the Admiral's meddling in the Dartmouth Diaries, Book Two: *Sweet Victory*, Book Three: *All For Victory*, Book Four: *Chasing Victory* and Book Five: Lasting Victory are also available on Amazon as well as my series of cosy mysteries involving the Admiral and Jimmy, aptly titled *The Admiral Shackleford Mysteries.*

Book One: *A Murderous Valentine*, Book Two: *A Murderous Marriage* and Book Three: *A Murderous Season* are all available on Amazon.

You might also be interested to learn that the Admiral's Great, Great, Great, Great, Great, Great Grandfather appears in my latest series of lighthearted Regency Romances entitled The Shackleford Sisters.

Book One: *Grace*, Book Two: *Temperance*, Book Three: *Faith* , Book Four: *Hope,* and Book Five: *Patience* are currently available on Amazon with Book Six: Charity to be released on 23rd February 2023.

Turn the page for a full list of my books available on Amazon.

Books available on Amazon

The Dartmouth Diaries:

Book 1 - Claiming Victory
Book 2 - Sweet Victory
Book 3 - All for Victory
Book 4 - Chasing Victory
Book 5 - Lasting Victory

The Admiral Shackleford Mysteries

Book 1 - A Murderous Valentine
Book 2 -A Murderous Marriage
Book 3 - A Murderous Season

The Shackleford Sisters
Book 1- Grace
Book 2 - Temperance
Book 3 - Faith
Book 4 - Hope
Book 5 - Patience
Book 6 - Charity to be released on 23rd Feb 2023

Standalone Titles
An Officer and a Gentleman Wanted

About The Author

Beverley Watts

Beverley and her husband live in an apartment overlooking the sea on the beautiful English Riviera.

Between them they have 3 adult children and two gorgeous grandchildren plus a menagerie of animals including 4 dogs - 2 Romanian rescues of indeterminate breed called Florence and Trixie, a neurotic 'Chorkie' named Pepé and a 'Chichon" named Dotty who was the inspiration for Dotty in The Dartmouth Diaries. They also have a cat called Honey.

Beverley spent 8 years teaching English as a Foreign Language to International Military Students in Britannia Royal Naval College which is the premier officer training establishment for the Royal Navy in the UK. She says that in the whole 8 years there was never a dull moment and many of her wonderful experiences at the College were not only memorable but were most definitely 'the stuff of fiction'

An avid reader and writer since childhood, she always determined that on leaving she would write a book. Her debut novel An Officer And A Gentleman Wanted is very loosely based on her adventures at the College.

Beverley has written a series of romantic comedies entitled The

Dartmouth Diaries. Claiming Victory: Book One, Sweet Victory: Book Two, All For Victory: Book Three, Chasing Victory: Book Four, and Lasting Victory: Book Five are available on Amazon.

The first three books of her Admiral Shackleford Cozy Mystery series - A Murderous Valentine, A Murderous Marriage and A Murderous Season - are also available on Amazon.

Beverley has now embarked on a new series of Regency Romantic Comedies entitled The Shackleford Sisters. Book One: Grace, Book Two: Temperance, Book Three: Faith, Book Four: Hope and Book Five: Patience are available on Amazon. Book Six: Charity will be released on 23rd February 2023.

Printed in Great Britain
by Amazon

12156761R00119